Here's what readers ~~i~~ country are saying abou~~t~~ AMERICAN CH~~...~~

"I have 23 of your books, but INCREDIBLE IVY OF IOWA is my very favorite. I've read it five times!"

-Conner P., age 11, Iowa

"Thanks for coming to our school! Everyone thought you were going to be really scary, but you were really funny. Come back next year!"

-Caroline M., 12, Arizona

"I get so freaked out when I read your books, but I can't stop!"

-Jack T., age 10, Florida

"Did all of these things that you write about really happen to you? My sister says they're all true stories, but she lies about everything."

-Thad A., Age 11, California

"MUTANT MAMMOTHS OF MONTANA was awesome! I'm from Montana, and that book was super-cool! Will you write another one about my state?"

-Shelley R., age 9, Montana

"I read about your camp at the back of one of your books, and I'm going to go when I get old enough. I love to write, and I can't wait!"

-Jordyn T., age 8, Illinois

"I have to tell you that you're my favorite author! I never liked reading before, until I read IDAHO ICE BEAST. I loved that book, and I even did a book report on it!"

-Mark R., age 10, Oregon

"Your dogs are so cute. Your books are good, but I like your dogs, too. You should write a book about them."

-Jasmine J., age 13, South Carolina

"I know you get a ton of mail, but I hope you read this. Everyone in my school is in love with your books! Our library has a bunch of them, but they're never on the shelves when I go to get another one."

-Preston N., age 9, Michigan

"We had a book fair at our school, and they had a bunch of your books. I bought three of them and I read all of them! They're great! I'm going to buy more when we have another book fair."

-Rachel S., age 11, Pennsylvania

"We took a vacation and went to Chillermania and you were there! Do you remember me? My name is Bryson, and I had blue shirt. I bought six books and a hat! My dad says we will come again next summer."

-Sam W., age 12, Tennessee

"Keep writing! I love all of your books, especially the Michigan Chillers, because that's where I'm from!"

-Aaron P., age 10, Michigan

Chill Out, Dyson!

SAULT STE. MARIE SEA MONSTERS

"Thank you for writing me back! My friends didn't believe you would, but I showed them your letter and the bookmark you sent. That was so cool!"

-Kate B., age 10, Indiana

"My favorite book is SAVAGE DINOSAURS OF SOUTH DAKOTA. I think you should make movies out of all your books, especially this one!"

-Keith A., Age 11, New Jersey

"I started reading the Freddie Fernortner books, and now I'm reading all of your American Chillers books! I love all of them! I can't decide which one is my favorite."

-Jenna T., age 9, Minnesota

"After I read VIRTUAL VAMPIRES OF VERMONT, I had strange dreams. Does that happen to anyone else, or is it just me?"

-Anders B., age 12, Texas

"I read your books every night just before I go to bed. I have six of my own, but I borrow more from the library. I love all of them! Keep writing!"

-Annette O., age 11, Nebraska

Got something cool to say about Johnathan Rand's books? Let us know, and we might publish it right here! Send your short blurb to:

Chiller Blurbs
281 Cool Blurbs Ave.
Topinabee, MI 49791

Other books by Johnathan Rand:

#18: Sault Ste. Marie
Sea Monsters

Johnathan Rand

An AudioCraft Publishing, Inc. book

This book is a work of fiction. Names, places, characters and incidents are used fictitiously, or are products of the author's very active imagination.

Book storage and warehouses provided by Chillermania!©
Indian River, Michigan

Michigan Chillers #18: Sault Ste. Marie Sea Monsters
ISBN 13-digit: 978-1-893699-20-5

Librarians/Media Specialists:
PCIP/MARC records available **free of charge** at
www.americanchillers.com

Cover illustration by Dwayne Harris
Cover layout and design by Sue Harring

Printed in USA

SAULT STE. MARIE
SEA MONSTERS

VISIT CHILLERMANIA!

WORLD HEADQUARTERS FOR BOOKS BY JOHNATHAN RAND!

CHILLERMANIA!

**I-75 Exit 313
then south
1 mile!**

Visit the HOME for books by Johnathan Rand! Featuring books, hats, shirts, bookmarks and other cool stuff not available anywhere else in the world! Plus, watch the American Chillers website for news of special events and signings at *CHILLERMANIA!* with author Johnathan Rand! Located in northern lower Michigan, on I-75! Take exit 313 . . . then south 1 mile! For more info, call (231) 238-0338. And be afraid! Be veeeery afraaaaaaiiiid . . . .

1

It was the perfect summer day, and I mean absolutely, one-hundred percent *perfect.* The sun was shining, there were only a few breaths of feathery clouds in the sky, and the temperature was near eighty.

And my new best friend, Zach Kuschman, and I were at Sherman Park with dozens of other people who were doing the same thing as us: soaking up the sun; relaxing on huge, colorful towels; and swimming in the cool, rich waters of the wide St. Mary's River. But then the heat became too much for us to take.

"Man, I need to get a drink of water," Zach

said. He rolled to his knees on the beach towel and stood, momentarily blocking the harsh sun and covering me with a deliciously cool shadow. "Want me to bring you back something?"

"I'll take a vanilla ice cream cone with two scoops, fudge, and candy sprinkles on top," I said with a smile.

Zach smirked. "Sorry," he said. "Best I can do is bring you a water or a lemonade. I think that's all my mom packed in the cooler."

"I'll take a lemonade if you have an extra," I said.

Zach thrust out his thumb and winked. "All right, Rock," he said. "Be right back."

That's what he calls me: Rock. My name is really Brittany Rockensuess, but Zach has taken to calling me 'Rock.' I don't mind at all. Actually, I kind of like the nickname.

"I'll be here," I replied, and his shadow fell away from me. Once again, the hot sun baked my skin, and I gave my arms, legs, and stomach a quick glance to make sure I wasn't getting burned.

I'd reapplied more sunscreen after my last swim, but I didn't want to take any chances.

If only my friends could see me now, I thought, *here beneath the hot sun, over a thousand miles from where they were right now.*

It's kind of funny: when I told my friends in Texas—that's where we used to live—that my family was moving to Michigan, they freaked out.

"Michigan?!?!" they all said. "Isn't Michigan like the snow capital of the *world?*" All my friends warned me that I was going to freeze to death beneath a mountain of ice or die in a raging blizzard.

Of course, Michigan *does* get a lot of snow, especially where we live in Sault Sainte Marie, or 'The Soo,' as it's often called. It's a small city that borders Canada in Michigan's Upper Peninsula. Sault Sainte Marie in French means 'The Rapids of St. Mary,' and the only thing separating the two countries is the St. Mary's River, which connects Lake Superior to the west and Lake Huron to the east. Also separating the two countries is the

International Bridge, where thousands of cars and trucks travel between the two countries every day. In fact, The Soo is actually *two* cities. There is Sault Sainte Marie, Michigan, and Sault Sainte Marie, Canada. It's kind of cool knowing that we can get in the car and drive to another country in just a few minutes, simply by crossing a bridge.

And although the word is actually 'Sainte,' it's hardly ever spelled that way. It's always abbreviated. So, whenever you see it on a map or anywhere, you'll almost always see it as 'Sault Ste. Marie.'

Something else that Sault Ste. Marie is famous for is what's known as the Soo Locks. It's a system in the St. Mary's River that is used to 'lock' big freighters and other boats in a confined space, and lower or raise the water level so the ships can pass through. This is because the water level of Lake Superior is higher than the other Great Lakes, so the lock system is used to keep ships in a space of the river where the contained water level can be lowered or raised. Of course, it's a lot more technical than that, but that's how it was explained to me by my mom when I asked her about it. Lots of people come from all over to see giant freighters pass through the locks to get from Lake Superior to Lake Huron, and it's pretty cool. I took some pictures of the lock system and sent them to my friends in Texas.

But what my friends didn't know was that while Michigan *does* get a lot of snow, the summers are spectacular. It gets hot, too. Not quite as hot as Texas. And in Michigan, there's water just about everywhere. Lakes, creeks, ponds, streams . . . you name it. Beaches and places to swim are all over the place. That's something Texas doesn't have a lot of, except for the coastal areas in the southern part of the state. I think my friends in Texas would like Michigan in the summer, but I don't think they'd care for the winters too much. They were right about that: Michigan winters *can* be extremely cold, and there's always a ton of snow.

But right now, it was summer. It was

summer, I was on the beach at Sherman Park with my best friend, and the day was sunny and hot. Everything about the afternoon was absolutely perfect . . . until a man wading in the water near the shore began screaming.

The man's screaming made everyone turn their heads. The beach was really crowded, too, with lots of people in the sand and a bunch of people in the water. But when the man began wailing, everyone stopped and stared in his direction, including me.

Not far from shore, in knee-deep water, a man about my dad's age wearing bright red swim trunks was balancing on one leg. He held his other foot in both hands. Even from a distance, I could see why he was screaming: his leg and foot were covered in blood!

What I *didn't* see was Zach returning with two cans of lemonade.

"Is that blood on that dude's foot out there?" Zach asked as he sat on the blanket.

"I think so," I said, taking one of the cans of lemonade in my hand. "I wonder what happened."

We stared at the man in the water, holding his foot just above the small waves. He lost his balance once and had to drop his injured leg into the water, and then he limped toward the shore where several people rushed to help him.

"Maybe he was attacked by a shark," Zach said with a chuckle.

"There aren't any sharks in the St. Mary's River," I said, rolling my eyes. "And there aren't any in the Great Lakes, either."

"Hey," Zach said, taking a short sip of his lemonade. "You never know. There was that kid a few years back that found a real megalodon tooth on the shore of Lake Huron. In fact, that one guy wrote a book about a freshwater megalodon that lived in a lake in Mississippi."

"I read that book," I said. "That guy who wrote it just made it up. He wrote a bunch of scary books like that. It's just his weird imagination."

"Maybe so," Zach said. "But that book made me think twice before I got in the water again."

The injured man had reached the beach, and a woman was helping him walk. I could hear chattering, but because we were so far away, I could only make out pieces of words and sentence fragments like 'sharp rock,' 'bad cut,' and 'stitches.'

"Looks like he's going to be okay," I said. "Sounds like he cut his foot on a rock."

"Good thing he's out of the water," Zach said. "All that blood is bound to attract more sharks."

I smiled and leaned back onto the towel. That's one of the reasons I like Zach so much: he's got a great sense of humor. He's not sarcastic or mean or anything; not like that at all. He just has a funny way of looking at things, and he makes me laugh. I was glad to have him as a friend because of that.

But I was also glad to have him as a friend for other reasons . . . because the awful terror we were about to experience wasn't something anyone would want to go through alone.

We moved from Texas to Michigan in the fall of last year, when my dad got a job at a new factory in Sault Ste. Marie. He's a chemical engineer, and while I don't know a lot about what he does, I know he's pretty smart. But not as smart as Mom. Dad is always losing things around the house, and he can never find them. Mom knows where everything is, always. It's like she's psychic or something.

I have a little sister, too. Bella is only two years old, and I *adore* her. She's fun to play around with, and she has the cutest, goofiest smile you've ever seen.

We also have a cat named Dora. She showed up on our doorstep a few days after we moved to our new home in Michigan. We couldn't find her owner. Dad put an ad in the paper, and I made signs and posted them up and down our street, but nobody responded. So, we decided to keep her. She pretty much keeps to herself, but she's playful when she wants to be. I named her Dora, and she and Bella are best pals.

I met Zach on the same day we moved in. He was riding by on his bike when he saw Mom, Dad, and me carrying things into the house. Bella was playing in the yard with a doll. Zach turned around, stopped his bike, and asked Dad if we needed help. Dad thought that was pretty cool: that a stranger would ask if he could help out. I, too, thought it was nice of him. Zach helped all day, until the last box was carried inside from the truck. We've been best friends ever since.

"You know," Zach said as we watched the

man being helped across the beach by a couple of people, "I was only kidding about sharks."

I smirked. "I know that," I said.

"But last week, there were some reports of some sort of strange fish or creature or monster in the hydroelectric canal, the section of the river that runs through the city."

That's another thing about the river: it's actually divided into two sections. There's the river to the north of the city that contains the Soo Locks and a smaller, narrower section that needles through the heart of the city. Both passageways reconnect to form a wide berth, which flows into Lake Huron. But the hydroelectric canal is dammed up at the east and west sides. Fish can get through to the river, but not boats.

I rolled to my side, raising my arm to shield my eyes from the sun, so I could see Zach better.

"What sort of monster?" I asked with a grin, knowing that he was going to come up with some crazy story.

"You didn't hear about it?" Zach asked. He

sounded serious.

I shook my head, still smiling, still waiting for the punchline of the joke. "Nope," I replied.

"I know it sounds weird," Zach said. "But a few people said they saw something strange in the water. There was even a reporter from the newspaper who saw it, and he did a story about it."

"What did he see?" I asked.

Zach shrugged. "He wasn't sure himself. He said it was like a huge shadow beneath the surface of the river, near the locks. It made a big wake. Whatever it was, he said it was too big to be a normal fish. He said that it might have had a human-type shape, but he couldn't be sure. He was pretty freaked out by it."

"Maybe it was the Soo Locks Monster," I said with a smile. "You know . . . sort of like the Loch Ness Monster, only living here, in the waters between the United States and Canada."

"That would be cool," Zach said, and he gazed out over the clear, blue waters of the St.

Mary's River, at the dark strip of land a couple of miles to the north that is Canada. "Think about it," he continued. "A real sea monster, living in Lake Superior or in the St. Mary's River."

"No," I said, rolling to a sitting position and scanning the waters. "I don't think it would be cool at all. I think it would be *scary.*"

"Well," Zach said as he fell back onto the towel. "I don't think we have anything to worry about. You know how people tend to make things up. I don't think there *is* such a monster. But Lake Superior *is* pretty deep. You never know what might be lurking down there, just waiting for a chance to gobble someone up."

Of course, I didn't believe it, either. Sea monsters aren't real.

But I was wrong. I was wrong, and my first summer in Sault Ste. Marie, Michigan, was about to become a real-life horror story.

4

A few days went by. The weather became kind of pukey, and the temperature sank. Rain fell on and off, too, and the sky was gray and dull. I talked to Zach on the phone, but we didn't get together.

But one day Zach sent me a text, wanting me to call him right away. Of course, if it was something important, I don't know why he didn't call me in the first place.

I punched the return call icon and pressed the phone to my ear. It rang once, and then Zach's gritty voice squawked in my ear.

"Rock! You ready for this?!?!"

I pulled the phone away and winced, surprised by the loudness and excitement of his voice. I smiled and laughed as I cautiously returned the phone to my ear.

"Ready for *what?*" I replied.

"My uncle has two new kayaks! He says we can use them while he goes on a business trip! Wanna go?"

"Yeah!" I said. But then, I thought about it. "I've never been in a kayak before," I said.

"They're a cinch," Zach said. "Really easy. These are the kind you can sit or kneel in. We can take them out to the beach and cruise around in the water. It'll be cool!"

"That sounds awesome!" I said, unable to contain my excitement. "When?"

"As soon as it gets warm again," Zach said. "My mom says tomorrow is supposed to be a nice day. How about you meet me over here at my house at ten tomorrow morning?"

"Perfect!" I said.

I ended the call, excited about learning how to kayak, excited about exploring the deeper water beyond the beach, excited about another adventure. I'll admit I was a little fearful of the kayak, but that was only because I'd never been in one before. I'd heard it was easy to tip over in a kayak. However, Zach said I'd learn fast, and I believed him. So, my fear about kayaking was quickly erased by my excitement and enthusiasm of learning something new and different.

I went to bed that night wondering what it was going to be like, wondering how fun it would be. I was so focused on kayaking with Zach that I'd forgotten all about the mysterious sightings of the underwater creature in the river a few weeks before. The entire conversation with Zach had completely slipped my mind, as if it had been erased, as if it had never occurred. I never even *thought* about the strange creature in the water.

My memory would soon receive a horrifying jolt. And if I didn't believe that sea monsters existed in the depths of the Great Lakes, stalking the waters around Sault Ste. Marie, well, I was about to learn a lesson I wouldn't soon forget. That is, of course, if Zach and I survived our kayaking excursion and what would turn out to be one of the deadliest experiences of our lives.

The next morning, I was greeted by bright sunshine and a blue sky outside my window. Like the weather forecasters had predicted, the rain and cooler temperatures had moved on. I opened my bedroom window, and a fresh, warm breeze washed over my face and gently ruffled the curtains.

And it was Friday, the beginning of the weekend. Although school was out, and I had all summer to pretty much do what I wanted, I always looked forward to Saturday and Sunday, days that just seemed to be made for friends, family, and fun adventures.

And kayaking, I suddenly remembered.

I dressed quickly and gulped down a bowl of cereal. I retrieved my phone and my armband from my bedroom, both of which I received from my parents as a birthday gift. The phone is great, and the armband keeps it snug against my left arm, so I don't have to worry about carrying it.

Another great thing: my phone case is completely waterproof. If it gets rained on, or if I accidentally drop it in the water, it won't get ruined. Last summer at our home in Texas, Dad accidentally dropped his phone in our pool and fried it. He had to get a new one.

I bicycled over to Zach's house. The ride took only a few minutes, and I zipped into the driveway to find my friend waiting on the front porch. He was wearing blue shorts, a yellow tank top with a green cartoon frog on the front, and a wide smile that was as bright as the sun.

"Ready for some fun?" he asked, making a fist and giving the 'thumbs-up' sign.

I nodded and grinned. "For sure!" I replied. "But like I told you yesterday: I've never been in a kayak before."

Zach waved his hand carelessly. "Don't worry," he said. "You'll get the hang of it in seconds. It's easy, and it's a lot of fun."

And it was. In ten minutes, we were at the beach, where we met Zach's uncle. He'd brought the kayaks over in the back of his truck and unloaded them for us, telling us that he'd be back later in the afternoon to pick them up.

Five minutes later, we were paddling our kayaks away from the shore under the warmth of a lemony-sun and a blue sky with not a single cloud in sight. The kayak I was in was green; Zach's was red. Both were made of thick plastic and were light enough for each of us to pick up. We each slipped into orange life vests and fastened them tightly. Zach had given me some quick instructions on how to use the double-ended paddle, and we were off.

And just like he said, I got the hang of kayaking right away. It really *was* very easy. The narrow build of the kayak made it slip easily through the water, and the double-ended paddle with a blade on both ends made it easy to power and steer the small floating craft. I thought it was going to be difficult to balance, but I quickly got the hang of it.

This is even easier than learning how to ride a bike, I thought as I glided through the water next to Zach.

"Fun, huh?" Zach said with a wide smile.

I bobbed my head. "This is great!" I said. "I wish my friends in Texas could see me now!"

"Are you sure that thing is waterproof?" Zach asked.

"What thing?" I replied.

"Your phone," he said, and he motioned toward me with his paddle.

"Well, the phone itself isn't," I replied. "But the case is waterproof. It keeps the phone safe in case it gets dropped in water."

"My mom wouldn't let me bring mine," Zach said. "She said I might drop it in the river and ruin it or lose it."

We easily sliced through the water, bobbing and knifing through the low waves. The water beyond the park is very shallow for a long way out, and then it suddenly drops off and becomes deep. Where this happens, the water color seems to change from a dull blue-green to a deep, dark blue, and we could no longer see the bottom.

Zach paddled his kayak ahead of me, heading northwest. Far off, I could see a dark, green, horizontal strip of land: Canada.

And everything was perfect. The sun, the sky, the gentle wind, and the lazy waves. The distant laughing of seagulls in the sky.

Perfect.

That is, until Zach's kayak suddenly rolled sideways. Zach screamed and plunged into the water. His life vest had come off, and it floated near the overturned vessel. The paddle drifted next to it.

I wasn't alarmed . . . at first. At first, I expected to see his head pop up at any second. He would smile and laugh at his foolishness, and then climb back into his kayak.

A second went by.

Another.

Thirty seconds passed.

"Zach?" I called out. Which, of course, was pointless, as there was no way Zach would be able to hear me under the water.

A full minute passed, and a dark panic began to chew at my belly. Zach's kayak remained upside down. His life vest had drifted a dozen feet away, aimlessly rolling on the waves.

Zach was gone.

I could do just one of two things, and I had to make a split-second decision. I could call for help with my phone, or I could dive down and try to help Zach. I knew that if I called for help, the police—the marine patrol—would come.

But I also knew they would arrive far too late to do anything. In the time it took for anyone to reach us, Zach would have drowned.

So, in the flash of an instant, I decided to act. I unsnapped my life vest, took a deep breath—

And then my phone rang.

My ring tone is a very strange warble, not really a song, and it doesn't have a beat. I guess the only way to describe it is that it sounds like a robotic bird chirping. I found it online for free, and I thought it was cool and different.

Quickly, I glanced at the phone on my arm. I didn't recognize the number on the screen, so I ignored the call, dropped the paddle, twisted my body to the side, and rolled into the water.

Beneath the surface, I opened my eyes. Everything, of course, was fuzzy and hazy, out-of-focus. Curtains of light shimmered through green-blue fabric, fingering into the dark, forbidden depths.

And, oddly enough, I could hear my phone ringing beneath the surface. It sounded a little garbled, but I was surprised at how clear it sounded. I was glad for my waterproof case, too, or my phone would have been ruined.

But there wasn't any sign of Zach. He'd been wearing a yellow tank top, and I thought it would be easy to spot him under water. But the only thing I could see was the endless, dark blue mystery of the deep.

I kicked with my legs and pulled with my arms, slicing deeper through the water. I turned my head from side to side, all around.

My phone continued warbling while my eyes scanned the depths for Zach.

Nothing.

My mind was spinning, racing. *Where is he?!?! Where is he?!?!*

Fifteen seconds passed, and my phone continued to ring. I dived deeper, and I could feel pressure in my head around my ears.

Twenty seconds passed, and I still hadn't spotted Zach.

The dark panic that had been gnawing at my belly grew to a gut-piercing, tight horror. Zach had been under water for over a minute, and I knew that time was running out for him.

And time was running out for me, too. I knew that I couldn't hold my breath for much longer, and I'd have to surface. And when I did, I would have to face the fact that Zach was gone. Zach was gone, and I would have to call for help.

Help that, unfortunately, would arrive much, much too late.

Finally, my phone stopped ringing. And just when I was about to give up my search and rocket to the surface, a movement in the dark depths caught my attention.

Zach!

No.

No, it wasn't Zach.

My eyes bulged, and I nearly opened my mouth to scream.

In the murky depths below me was a hideous thing, a monster of some sort, with huge eyes and scales and arms and legs, reaching out, reaching up, reaching for me . . . .

Panic and fear tore through my mind, and I turned. I kicked hard and pulled with my arms, reaching for the bright surface above, knowing that at any second, I would feel the tight grasp of the sea monster grabbing at my legs or perhaps feel his teeth tearing and ripping at my soft skin and flesh.

I exploded to the surface, screaming and gasping, splashing furiously. My green kayak floated nearby, and Zach's red kayak drifted a few feet beyond.

"Rock?!?!" I heard a voice shout.

It was Zach!

"Zach!" I screamed, still thrashing in the waves, treading on the surface. My head snapped around, back and forth, searching for the monster that, I knew, would surface at any moment or grab me by the legs and pull me under. "Zach! Where *are* you?!?!"

"I'm right here!" Zach called out.

And suddenly, I could see him. He'd been on the other side of his kayak, in the water, his head hidden from view by the small craft.

"What's the matter?" he said, and he began crawling through the water, arm over arm, toward me.

I, however, wasn't going to wait for him to reach me. Using every available muscle, every ounce of strength, I flailed and pulled and kicked and twisted toward my kayak. I reached it in seconds and pulled myself up, which was a bit tricky, because the kayak rolled easily.

But I managed. Carefully, but quickly, I crawled into my kayak, my lungs burning, my breath heaving. The paddle had been drifting next to it, and I plucked it from the water and placed it on my lap.

Zach was only a few feet away. When he finally reached my kayak, he grabbed the sides of it to steady himself in the water.

"Hey, calm down," he said. "It was just a joke. I was hiding from you on the other side of my kayak. I didn't think you'd freak out so much."

I shook my head and thought I was going to cry.

"Not you," I said, still gasping and hacking. "There—there's something in the water. *There's something in the water!*"

Zach looked down, searching the water around him.

"Like what?" he asked. "A fish?"

"No!" I screamed. I was nearly crying. "It was some sort of monster! Get in the kayak, quick, before he gets you!"

Zach grinned. "A monster?" he replied.

"I'm not kidding!" I said. "I dove down to look for you, and I saw some . . . some . . . *thing!* I don't know what it was! It was huge, and it was

43

ugly. And it was coming to get me!"

"Take it easy," Zach said. "There's nothing in the water that will bother you. You probably saw a big fish. Maybe a sturgeon. They get huge. Bigger than you, even. But they don't hurt anyone."

"It wasn't a *fish!*" I insisted. "It was some sort of weird sea monster!"

"There's no such thing as sea monsters," Zach said.

"But you told me that someone saw something in the river not far from here!" I replied. I was shouting. "You said a newspaper reporter wrote a story about it."

"Yeah, but he really didn't *see* anything. Just a dark form in the water and a wake. It was probably just a fish or something."

"I don't know what I saw, but it was *there!* I saw it with my own eyes!"

Again, Zach looked around. "Well," he said, "I don't see anything. It's gone now."

My life vest had been bobbing nearby in the waves. Zach grabbed it and handed it to me.

"Why did you do that?!?!" I asked. Now that

I was okay, and I knew that Zach hadn't drowned, my fear was turning to anger. "Why did you play a trick like that?"

"Hey, hey, I'm sorry," Zach replied. "I really am. I thought it would be funny. I guess it wasn't."

"No, it wasn't!" I snapped. "If you do that and you're just playing a joke like that, no one is going to help you when you really need it. Haven't you ever heard the story of the boy who cried 'wolf?'"

"Yeah, I guess you're right," Zach said. "I guess that wasn't a very smart prank."

"No, it wasn't," I said.

While Zach swam back to his kayak, I slipped into my life vest and fastened the black plastic buckles. I looked around at the blue sky, at the rich, Canadian land mass to the north and the shining beach of Sherman Park on the American side, much closer, to the south.

I rested the double-bladed paddle on my legs and looked down into the shimmering depths, half expecting to see the creature—whatever it was—coming up at me, lunging toward the surface, flipping my kayak and launching me into the water where it would grab me and pull me under.

But the creature never came.

Maybe Zach is right, I thought. *Maybe it was just a fish. Or my imagination.*

There's no such thing as sea monsters, Zach had said.

And he should know. He'd lived in the Soo all his life. Despite the reports of a strange monster in the St. Mary's River, sea monsters exist only in books and movies, right?

Right?

Wrong.

And my summer of fear was about to begin.

"Check this out," Zach said, walking up to our front porch. He'd ridden his bike to our house, dropped it in the grass, and was nearly running toward me. In his hand was his phone.

"What is it?" I asked.

"I'll let you decide. Check this out!"

A few days had passed since our kayaking adventure, since I'd spotted the horrifying creature—whatever it was—beneath the surface. I had told my mom and dad about it, but they said the same thing Zach had said: that it was probably just a big fish.

Sea monsters aren't real, they told me.

He held out his phone, and I shaded the screen with my hand to block the harsh sunlight. At first, I couldn't make out the image.

"What is it?" I asked again.

"It's a picture that was taken yesterday by the mouth of the St. Mary's River, near the Soo Locks. A guy in a big freighter spotted something in the water, and this is the picture he took."

I continued to look, but the bright sun caused too much screen glare. I leaned to the side and drew closer to the phone.

Suddenly, I could make out the image.

I froze, and my eyes nearly popped out of my head. I drew a single, sharp breath, half a gasp, and held it. Then, I snatched the phone from Zach's hand and held it closer to my face.

The image was simple: it was a photo of water and waves, hazy blue and shimmering in the sun. And in the middle of the photo: a dark shadow. Although it was blurry and small, it was unmistakably a creature of some sort, just breaking the surface. I could make out two arms and a head with dark, menacing eyes.

"That's what I saw in the water the other day!" I said. "That has to be the same thing!"

"It's kind of blurry," Zach replied. "You can't really see much."

"But look," I said, and I pointed to the screen. "There are two arms and a head, right there. There's no *way* that's a fish!"

Zach shrugged. "It might be," he said.

I was incredulous. "What do you mean?" I said. "That's not a *fish!* Fish don't have arms like that!"

"It's too blurry," Zach said, holding the screen to his face for a closer inspection. "I mean, there's obviously something there, but you can't really make out what it is, other than a dark shape of some sort."

I looked again. I supposed that if you hadn't seen the same nightmarish vision I had, if you hadn't spotted the mysterious creature in the murky depths, well, the blurry photo probably wouldn't mean much. And I had to admit that maybe—*just maybe*—the image in the picture wasn't anything at all. It could have been a log or some other piece of floating junk that just *looked* like a creature of some sort.

But I knew better.

"Well, whatever it is," Zach said, "people are talking about it all over town. Some people are really freaked out, but others just think it's a hoax."

"Well," I said, "I don't know about the picture, but I *know* what I *saw*. I saw a sea monster."

"Want to go kayaking again?" Zach asked with a smirk.

"Are you nuts?" I replied. "I don't think I'm ever going back in the water again. Not with that—that—*thing* out there."

Zach smiled. "I kinda figured. But let's go to the park, anyway. We don't have to go in the water. It's a hot day, and it'll be a lot of fun."

I agreed. The day was hot, and hanging out at the park seemed like a great idea.

It wasn't.

Sherman Park was packed; there were people everywhere. With the day so beautiful and hot, Zach and I weren't the only ones who thought it would be a great place to spend the day. Families grilled food and had lunch in the picnic area, and dozens of people splashed in the cool, clean waters. Broken bits of music drifted on the breeze like puzzle pieces, and the glaring, yellow sun watched from her perch, slowly trekking west across the sky.

But it wasn't long before a mild panic broke

out.

Like Zach had said, many people were talking about the mysterious shadow in the photo that had been taken the day before. The image had been reproduced in the newspaper, shared on the Internet, and even the local television news was talking about it. At the park, we overheard many people discussing the photo, imagining out loud what the image could possibly be. Some people seemed convinced it was some sort of prehistoric water beast, but an equal number of people thought it was nothing more than a trick of light or a shadow. Some thought it was nothing more than a cheap hoax.

But other people, more dedicated, were looking for the creature in the river. I saw people standing at the edge of the beach a few feet from the water, gazing out across the glimmering surface, hoping to see something. I have to admit that I, too, cast a few wary glances at the river, but I saw nothing but happy people laughing and splashing and swimming. Not far away, a group of college kids had set up a net in the shallows and were having a great time playing volleyball. If they were worried about a sea monster, it certainly didn't show.

"I don't think anyone is going to see anything," Zach said. He'd reached into his cooler, grabbed a couple of cold cans of lemonade, and handed one to me.

"What do you mean?" I asked. The breeze toyed with my hair, and a lock fell over my eyes. I reached up and pulled it aside.

Zach motioned with his drink, dipping it toward several people who'd taken up sentry in the park, staring at the water. Two people held binoculars to their faces, scanning the waves.

"I'll bet those people won't see anything," Zach said. "I mean, if I were a sea monster, I wouldn't show up at the beach on a sunny day."

"Why?" I asked.

Zach shook his head. "Too many people," he replied. He spoke slower, his voice dripping with tension and drama. "I'd want to stay hidden, stay in deep water where no one would see me." He wedged his can of lemonade in the sand and raised his arms, making claws with his hands. "Then, at night, when everyone was asleep, I would sneak to shore, roam the neighborhood, and snare my next victim."

I rolled my eyes and laughed. "You make it sound like a movie," I said.

But I had to admit that the idea of some strange monster lurking in the water was more than a bit frightening to me. I hadn't said anything to Zach, but I was nervous about going kayaking again, or even going near the water. I was nervous enough just sitting in the sand at Sherman Park. Call me silly or paranoid or whatever, but it just didn't seem safe.

Come on, Brittany, I thought. *Maybe you just imagined it.*

No.

Yes.

No. I know what I saw.

Yes!

Yes?

It was strange, having an argument with yourself inside your head, two identical voices with different opinions, with different positions on the same topic.

Okay.

Okay, so maybe what I saw in the depths that day *was* my imagination. Maybe there wasn't anything there, after all. Maybe—

My thoughts were interrupted by a woman screaming. The shrill sound snagged my attention, and I turned. Zach spun, too, and I quickly saw that many other people had done the same.

"There he is!" a woman with binoculars screeched. *"The sea monster! He's out there right now!"*

Zach and I looked at where she was pointing, out into the river. Others around us were pausing their activities to do the same thing.

"Do you see anything?" Zach asked.

I scanned the water and the throngs of people all around. The woman had returned the binoculars to her face, holding them to her eyes with one hand. With the other, she pointed.

I shook my head. "No," I said to Zach. "I don't see anything."

Tense moments flew by. Eyes were glued to

the water.

"There's nothing there," someone said.

"I don't see anything at all," said another.

The woman who'd shouted lowered her binoculars, keeping her attention on the water. "I'm telling you," she insisted, "he was right out there! I saw something in the water!"

And then, we *did* see something. Far out in the river, a black dot appeared.

A bird. Specifically, an aquatic bird called a cormorant. They swim underwater and eat fish, and they can get pretty big, nearly twice the size of seagulls.

Several people groaned and grumbled. Zach laughed.

"There's your sea monster, right there!" an older man chuckled. "Don't get too close, he might gobble you up!"

The woman with the binoculars frowned in frustration, but she didn't say anything. She simply continued scanning the water while people returned their attention to whatever they had been doing.

"So much for a sea monster," Zach said.

"But maybe she really *did* see something," I replied.

"I think the only thing she saw was one of those nasty birds," Zach said. "At least, that's what my dad calls them. 'Nasty birds.' He says those cormorants are eating all the fish."

"Maybe she saw something else," I said, still searching the water.

"I doubt it," Zach said. "Come on. It's hot. Let's get some ice cream."

I, however, was still glued to the wide river, hypnotized. I didn't know why. For some reason, things just seemed *too* perfect. The sunny day, the people, the kids playing in the sand and the water. Everything seemed like the glossy photo in a travel magazine, where all of the people are models with big smiles and perfect hair and colorful clothing, skin glistening with sunscreen and hopeful, exciting looks in their eyes. In their world, the perfect world of advertising, nothing ever went wrong.

And far out in the river, I saw a big freighter

slowly making its way to the Soo Locks, where it would carefully needle through and emerge from the other side to continue its journey down the St. Mary's River into Lake Huron and through the Great Lakes. From where I stood, the freighter barely seemed to be moving at all. It was just crawling along, plodding slowly through the waves.

But there was something familiar about the way it moved, slow and deliberate. Something I could relate to, but I guess I didn't realize it at the time. Later, however, I would realize that the big ship would symbolize what was going on in my life at that moment, what I was feeling at the time.

A slow-moving horror was coursing through the rivers of my bloodstream, just like the freighter. This fear, like the ship, was moving closer to its destination, churning along on its journey, unstoppable. I had felt this terror the day Zach played his prank on me, the moment I'd spotted the creature beneath the surface, looking up at me from the murky depths. That nagging fear had never left. Despite my attempts to push it away, to tell myself that I was being silly, that my fears were baseless, they were always there, day and night, wherever I went. Hiding beneath the surface of my skin, waiting.

I saw something in the water that day, something that wasn't my imagination. No matter how impossible it seemed, no matter how crazy it was, I *knew* what I had seen. Nobody could tell me any different.

I watched the freighter, slowly chugging through the river, pushing tons and tons of water out of its way.

Unstoppable.

And my fear was—

Unstoppable.

The terror was—

Real.

I *knew* it.

And within days, everyone in Sault Ste. Marie would know it, too.

11

A week went by, and nothing out of the ordinary happened. Zach and I hung out together a few times, went to the park, and explored some old trails and two-tracks. That's one thing that I loved about living in Sault Ste. Marie: there were lots of new places to explore, lots of forests and trails just beyond the city. So many that, if you weren't careful, you could easily get lost.

But Zach seemed to be familiar with most of these places, and he always told me not to worry. He said he knew his way around.

One evening, we rode our bikes into the city, stopped at a convenience store, and picked up a couple of candy bars. After we wolfed them down, we rode along East Portage Avenue, following it out of the city limits where Portage Avenue becomes Riverside Drive, a road that parallels the St. Mary's River. The river was on our left, to the east, and a warm breeze blew at us from our right, the west. Finally, when we reached Mission Creek, we stopped. The creek is small, but it widens as it opens and flows into the St. Mary's River. At this spot, a man was on the shore, holding a fishing pole.

"There are some big fish in the river," Zach said. He motioned toward the river and the man standing on shore. "When I was little, I caught a huge fish." He spread his arms. "I don't remember what kind it was, and it doesn't matter. But at the time, it seemed like it was bigger than me!"

"It doesn't look like he's catching much," I said, nodding toward the fisherman.

We got off our bikes and walked through the weeds down a short embankment. The man turned. Zach and I stopped walking.

"How's the fishing?" Zach asked.

The man shook his head without looking at us. "Just a few little ones," he replied. Then, he glanced at us and grinned. "Sure beats working, though."

Zach and I smiled back. "Have a nice day," I said.

"I will if I can catch—"

The man suddenly stopped speaking and pulled the fishing pole close to his chest. One hand was gripping the handle while the other held the crank. The rod was bent, arced like a rainbow, and looked as though it was ready to snap. The man struggled to hold it.

"Holy cow!" the man said. *"I think I've got a whale on here!"*

Oh, it wasn't a whale, that was for sure. What he had hooked was much, much worse.

12

Zach and I waded through the weeds and stopped next to the man. He held tightly to his fishing pole, which was bent and pulsating in quick, jerky movements.

"I've got a real monster this time!" the man said. Zach and I looked at each other. What the man meant, of course, was that he thought he'd hooked a big fish, and he was using the word 'monster' to describe it. But the word, to me, was literal. When he said the words 'real monster,' he had no idea that what he might have on the other end of his line might be just that—a monster.

"If . . . if I can get this . . . this thing to the shore, can you kids give me a hand landing him?" As he wrestled with his fishing pole, he struggled to speak. "I . . . I didn't bring . . . a . . . a net. Didn't think I'd be catching . . . anything this big!"

I looked at Zach, shook my head, and mouthed the word 'no.' Zach, however, only smirked at me and shrugged.

"Sure," he said to the man. "If he doesn't break your line first."

Whatever the fisherman had hooked, monster or fish, it hadn't yet broken the surface. All we could see was the spot where the clear monofilament line vanished into the water. And although the water was clean and clear, we couldn't see beneath the surface because of the glare of the sun on the water.

In the river, not far from shore, water churned and boiled. Whatever the man had hooked, it was getting closer to the surface.

My fear was swelling, and I suddenly remembered the big freighter I'd spotted a few days before and how it seemed to move like my fears. Only now, it seemed to be moving faster. In my mind, I saw the massive ship steaming full speed directly toward me, creating massive waves as it bore down, gigantic and unstoppable.

In the river, water boiled and churned on the surface again as the man continued to crank the fishing reel and fight with his catch. Whatever he'd hooked was getting closer.

"I can't believe he . . . he hasn't broken my line," the man said, still struggling to hold his bent fishing pole. "This has got to be the biggest fish in the river. Maybe . . . maybe even the Great Lakes!"

Zach took a few steps forward and crouched next to the river's edge. "Keep him coming!" he said to the man. "When he gets close to shore, I'll try to grab him!"

I wanted to shout to Zach, to scream at him, to tell him 'no,' to tell him to get back. I wanted to tell him that the man hadn't hooked a fish, but a terrible beast from the deep, dark depths, a creature that would tear us apart with long claws and incredible strength.

But the Great Freighter of Horror had frozen my vocal chords and locked my muscles in place. I couldn't speak; I couldn't move. All I could do was watch as the man reeled in his catch, as the enormous ship of horror pushed through my bloodstream, full steam ahead, coming straight for my soul.

Zach was kneeling near the edge of the river, arms out and ready. The man was standing behind him, fighting to hold the rod while reeling in the line, struggling to bring his catch closer and closer.

"Almost," Zach said. His eyes searched the canal. "I should be seeing him soon. Keep him coming . . . ."

"I'm having a hard . . . hard time holding on," the man said. "I sure do wish I would have brought a net."

Water churned.

"Almost," Zach repeated. "Bring him in easy. I'll try to grab him by the gills when he gets close to the shore."

Suddenly, the water directly in front of Zach

exploded in an eruption of black, foamy lava. The awful beast—the sea monster—burst from the water and stood upright at the river's edge, facing us in all his hideousness.

13

When the creature exploded from the water, the sudden surprise and disbelief caused the three of us to freeze. I think fear is like that sometimes. Sometimes, it takes a moment for your brain to register, to catch up and recognize what you're seeing—especially when it's something so incredibly unbelievable.

But very quickly, natural-born instinct takes over. It doesn't take the brain long to figure out that danger is very present and very real. The body's defense mechanism kicks in, telling our muscles what to do, how to react, how to respond.

But first, the brain needs to process all of the information it's being fed. It does this through what is being seen, heard, felt, and sensed.

And what we were seeing certainly wasn't a fish. It was a *monster*, a real, live, horrifying water beast. The same creature I'd spotted in the depths of the river a few weeks before. The same monster others had spotted; the same creature in the blurry photograph that had been shared on the Internet and published in the newspaper.

What we were seeing:

The creature had features like an adult human, but he was bigger. He had frog-like arms and legs, but they were longer, more like a salamander. His fingers were webbed, capped with short, curved talons. His thick, powerful arms were outstretched, and strands of dark, grimy seaweed hung from them like grimy tinsel on a Christmas tree.

And his head was human-like—sort of. It was bigger than a human head with the facial features of a prehistoric lizard: deep, dark, sunken eyes and a wide, reptilian mouth.

But perhaps the most striking feature was that the monster had no skin. Or maybe it *was* skin; I guess I couldn't tell. The beast was covered with what appeared to be large, plate-like scales, dark blue and black in color, glistening in the sun, water dripping from his webbed claws.

That was what my brain was registering; that was what I was taking in during that sudden, brief moment of surprise and shock.

And once the realization set in, once my mind figured out what was going on, it barked the order.

Run.

The fisherman heard the same order from his own brain. He threw down his pole, spun, and nearly knocked me over as he fled. Zach fell backward onto the ground, rolled to his side, and sprang to his feet. The fisherman took off one way, and Zach and I took off another. He and I ran through the weeds, stumbling up the embankment, not looking back, not wanting to see the horrible sea monster, afraid that it might be coming after us, that it might be right on our heels.

And while we were scrambling back to our bikes, an odd thought of victory fell over me.

I was right, I thought. *I was right all along. The sea monster is real. Now, Zach will have to believe me. He saw the sea monster with his own eyes. So did that fisherman.*

But my victorious thoughts gave way to relief when I finally did manage to glance over my shoulder.

The sea monster was gone. There were no ripples in the river, other than the normal fluctuation of the easy waves. A seagull swooped low through the sky, and a car passed by on Riverside Drive. Dark green trees stood motionless and silent, observing the day as it passed, basking beneath the evening sun as it made its way westward.

Zach and I were safe, and I was grateful for the relief I felt. I was grateful that the ugly creature, the horrible sea monster from the dark depths, wasn't coming after us. I was grateful that we'd all been able to get away without injury—or worse.

Unfortunately, it was a relief I wouldn't be feeling for very long.

14

Imagine this scene:

Four people sitting around a dinner table, two adults and two children. One adult, the large male, is totally engrossed in a newspaper. The adult female is passing around a large plate of steaming mashed potatoes. Both children, seated opposite one another, are girls. One is very small with a pink ribbon in her hair, and, with a stainless-steel fork, she is flinging cut green beans at a cat seated on the back of the couch in the living room. The cat, wide-eyed and amused, flinches every time a green bean flies past.

The other child is twelve, wolfing down food like she hasn't eaten in days. She is very animated. She is telling a bizarre story about a creature she'd spotted earlier in the day. She speaks quickly, her eyes are wide, and she uses both hands as she talks. The adults really don't believe her story. The adult male continues to read the paper without looking up, and the adult female smiles and nods while listening, all the while shuffling ceramic plates and plastic bowls, rearranging glasses and condiments to make space on the table. The little girl flinging the beans at the cat is grinning and could not care less about sea monsters.

The adult woman tells the small girl to stop flinging food.

The adult male continues reading the paper.

The older girl persists, waving her hands as she excitedly recites her story, insisting that it's true.

That girl is *me.*

"I'm serious!" I said for what was probably the tenth time. "You can call Zach and ask him. He was there. He saw the thing with his own eyes. So did the fisherman."

"I'm sure it was just a fish, Sweetheart," Mom said gently. "I've heard they grow pretty big in these parts." She glanced at Bella, who had just launched another green bean at Dora, narrowly missing the cat. "Bella! What did I just tell you?" Bella flashed a cute grin. Her eyes narrowed to slits, and her puffy cheeks swelled. She scooped up a giant spoonful of mashed potatoes and stuffed the creamy heap into her mouth.

"Fish don't have arms and legs," I replied.

"Fish domp hab arbs and lebs," Bella said, trying to mimic my words.

"Are you sure it wasn't a big frog?" Dad asked. He didn't look up from his newspaper.

"For the *last* time," I said, rolling my eyes and shaking my head, "it *wasn't* a frog! This thing was as big as you. Maybe bigger."

No matter what I said or how hard I tried, Mom and Dad wouldn't believe me. Finally, I gave up, resigned, and ate the rest of my dinner in silence.

Zach's parents had pretty much treated him the same way. He tried to explain to them what we'd seen, but they just told him it was his crazy imagination. They told him he was seeing things and that he should put his mind to better use by writing a book.

"I wish we knew who that fisherman was," I said to him. We were in front of my house, sitting on the curb next to the driveway. Two days had passed since the incident in the river at Mission Creek. The evening was warm and pleasant. The sun was going down, and shadows stretched across the lawn like flat statues. The air was filled with the delicious, heavy scents of barbecues and freshly-mowed grass.

Zach shook his head. "Doesn't matter," he replied. "I don't think anyone would believe him, either. I wish I would have thought to take a picture."

"Me, too," I said. "But I was too busy freaking out."

"Are you guys still going to the beach tomorrow?" Zach asked. I had told him that Dad had the day off from work, and my parents had planned a day at the beach. Normally, that would have sounded fun, and I would have been excited. But after what Zach and I had spotted in the river, I wasn't all that crazy about spending time near the water. And I certainly didn't plan on doing any swimming.

"Yeah," I said. "Can you make it?"

"I'd love to," Zach said. "That way, I can help you fight off the sea monster." He finished his sentence with a smirk, and I smiled, too.

"Want us to pick you up?" I asked.

Zach shook his head. "I'll just ride my bike over. I won't be able to stay all day, anyway. If I have my bike, I can leave and not have to get a lift home from your parents."

But I had a bad feeling about going to the beach. I had a feeling that something awful would happen. I tried to tell myself that nothing could go wrong, that even if there was such a thing as a sea monster, the chances of seeing him at the park were near zero.

That bad feeling stayed with me even when

I went to bed that night. It was with me the moment I awoke and while we packed for the day. It stayed with me in the car, and it was with me as we unloaded all our things and found a place in the sand at the beach.

That awful feeling became worse and worse as the day went on.

And then, just before noon, someone discovered enormous footprints in the sand by the water.

Zach and I were tossing a Frisbee back and forth, and my mom and Bella were splashing in the shallows. Dad was seated in a folding lawn chair, chatting on his phone. The day was sunny and hot, and many people had the same idea we did: pack a lunch for the day and hang out at the beach, beneath the hot sun and blue sky.

Suddenly, the air was filled with shouting from the far end of the beach. Two teenage boys were standing near the shore, pointing to their feet. They looked down and then up to eye level, waving their arms as if inviting every person at the park to come see what they'd found. Several people hurried toward them.

Zach caught the Frisbee I'd tossed and held it. He stared at the two boys who'd caused the commotion before turning to me and speaking. "Wonder what's up with them?" he asked.

Alarm bells were going off in my head. I could only imagine the worst. However, other than a crowd gathering, I didn't see anything out of the ordinary.

"I don't know," I said.

"Come on," said Zach. "Let's find out."

We walked through the hot sand toward the two boys. As we drew nearer, we could hear bits and pieces of words.

"Claws—"

"—Huge—"

"Monster—"

"—Big—"

Several dozen people had gathered around the two boys. All were staring at something on the ground, pointing, chatting excitedly. A park worker had arrived, and he was kneeling low, curiously inspecting the sand.

And when Zach and I saw what had attracted everyone's attention, we looked at one another, each seeing the black fear in the other's eyes.

There were large footprints in the sand, twice the size of a normal adult's footprint.

But maybe 'footprints' isn't the right word. They looked more like webbed claws, like huge duck prints with sharp knives digging into the wet sand. Whoever—or whatever—had made them was, no doubt, huge.

"Everyone take a step back," the park ranger said. "Don't mess up the tracks. We need to get a better look at these."

Reluctantly, the crowd widened as people backed up. Phones were pulled out, and pictures were snapped. For comparison, one man placed his foot next to a large claw mark in the sand. His footprint looked like a child's foot next to the monstrous track in the wet earth.

"I'll bet that thing we saw in town yesterday

made those tracks," I whispered, leaning closer to Zach so no one else would hear.

Zach nodded and spoke quietly. *"I'll bet you're right. That means he has to be around here somewhere, probably in the water."*

"But don't you see?" I asked. "He doesn't *have* to be in the water. He can come out of the water and can walk on land, on two feet. What kind of creature is he?"

Zach shook his head. "I don't know," he said. "But I sure would like to get another look at him."

He was about to get his wish.

16

Farther out in the river was a small sailboat. Its hull and sails gleamed white in the sun, and it looked like a perfect triangle bobbing on the water, pointing at the sky. A few other, smaller vessels—kayaks, dinghies, fishing boats, canoes, and paddleboards—drifted lazily in the late-morning sunshine. Far off, a freighter plodded eastward in the wide river, heading toward the Soo Locks.

Around us, the crowd had begun to disperse. People were falling away, holding their phones, talking excitedly to one another.

Then, someone shouted.

Zach and I looked up to see a woman pointing. Following her arm, we looked out into the river.

Something was happening on the small, white sailboat. From so far away, we couldn't tell exactly what was going on, but we saw a tiny, dark shadow hustling frantically about and then another. One of them dove into the water. Another person followed and then another.

By now, the beachgoers around us on the beach had turned to watch the commotion on the sailboat. There were gasps and whispers, and people held their phones up to take pictures.

"Look!" someone shouted. *"There it is!"*

A dark form appeared on the sailboat, but it was so far away we couldn't make out what it was. But I could tell that it was big . . . and I was certain it wasn't human.

"That's him!" I said to Zach. "That's the thing the fisherman reeled in yesterday in the river near Mission Creek! The same thing I saw in the water! It has to be!"

Zach didn't say anything. His hand was positioned above his forehead in a salute, shielding his eyes from the sun. He continued to gaze out over the river.

"Three of them are swimming to shore!" someone yelled. I could see three people in the water, their arms flailing wildy, as they pulled themselves through the water.

On the boat, however, the dark form of the monster reached up with a long, powerful claw and ripped the sail. A long tear formed in the white fabric, and it fluttered and whipped in the wind.

Then, the creature vanished.

On the beach, all around us, it was as if everyone was holding their breath. Although small waves continued to lap at the shoreline and gulls cried in the skies above, it was as if time had stopped.

No one spoke.

No one moved.

A lock of my hair fell over my eyes, tossed

by the wind. I pulled it back and looped it over my ear.

One by one, people began to speak. Some moved toward the water, waiting for the arrival of the three individuals frantically swimming toward shore. Two of them were wearing life vests, so their swimming was slow and cumbersome. The person without the life vest was able to move much faster in the water.

Farther out in the river, the sailboat with the torn sail bobbed lazily. No one was aboard to pilot it, and it was drifting aimlessly in the slow current.

There was no sign of the sea monster.

Then, without warning, the man who was not wearing the life vest yelled something—and vanished beneath the waves.

17

When the man went under, a dark, heavy gasp rolled through the crowd on the beach. However, the man was still so far away from shore that everyone knew there was no way anyone would be able to get to him in time.

Still, there were a couple of brave men who rushed into the water, racing into the waves, taking action, heading out to hopefully save the man who'd gone under.

However, their rescue efforts weren't necessary. Before any of the rescuers had a chance get in water deeper than their waists, the man who'd vanished popped back up again. He continued swimming toward the shore. The people who'd headed out to help him continued wading in the shallows to meet him as he arrived.

Farther out in the river, another boat showed up. Carefully, it plucked the other two survivors wearing life jackets from the water. From what I could see, they appeared to be okay.

Closer to shore, the other man, the man we'd watched go under and come back up, reached the shallows. Several people were there to meet him, grasping his arms and steadying him as he stood and waded toward shore. He was wearing khaki shorts and a white shirt that clung to his skin, dripping wet.

"It looks like everyone is safe," I said to Zach. "Unless there was someone else on the boat we don't know about."

Far out in the river, the rescue boat was approaching the damaged sailboat.

"I wouldn't go near that boat if I were them," I said. "Not with that thing out there."

The man who was being helped to shore was chattering wildly. Although we were too far away to hear everything he was saying, we heard the words 'sea monster' and 'attack' and 'ugly' and 'big.'

Zach looked at me. "Well," he said. "We were right. There really *is* a sea monster. Now, everyone else will know it, too."

"The question is," I replied, "where is he now? It doesn't look like he's on that sailboat anymore; otherwise, that other boat wouldn't go near it."

"He must have gone back into the river," Zach said. "That means he could be anywhere."

We scanned the wide expanse of the river, wondering if we might catch a glimpse of the creature's head, bobbing somewhere in the waves. We saw nothing, other than the normal sights and sounds of a normal summer day in a normal summer city in Michigan's Upper Peninsula. The sun glared down, baking the beach and heating the sand, its rays glistening on the water. In other parts of the park, people continued to play and enjoy themselves, either unaware of what had happened or too wrapped up in their own activities to care.

But soon, *everyone* in Sault Ste. Marie would know. Now that the creature had been spotted, now that it had attacked people and there had been witnesses, everyone in the Soo would be aware of the sea monster. And for everyone, it would be the beginning of a very, very bad dream.

A couple of things we learned at the beach later that day:

The man who'd gone under wasn't pulled beneath the waves by the sea monster. While he was swimming toward the beach, his wedding ring had slipped off his finger. He told people that he felt it fall off and dove down to retrieve it, but it was already too late. He said he caught a glimpse of it below him, a winking gleam of gold, as it sank into the depths and vanished. He hadn't been fast enough. Most likely, the wedding band was lost forever.

We also learned that nobody on the sailboat had been hurt. The police had arrived at the park, followed by an ambulance. The boat that had picked up the other two people from the water was met by a police boat in the river, and they were taken to the marina with the sailboat in tow. Everyone was safe, and, except for a bit of damage to the sailboat, everything was fine.

Except it *wasn't*. Nothing was fine. Nothing was fine at all.

For the next few days, the sea monster was the only thing people were talking about. It was in the newspapers, on television, on the radio, and all over social media. One of the people who had been on the sailboat described the monster as something that came out of an old monster movie from the 1950s. Some 'lagoon' monster, or something like that.

For a while, it seemed as though a sinister cloud had settled over Sault Ste. Marie. The idea that a hideous sea monster was lurking in the depths of the St. Mary's River or around the Great

Lakes had cast a dark shadow over the community and the surrounding region. Fear seemed to be everywhere.

A small group of people got together to form some sort of protection committee, saying that the creature should be left alone, to live in peace. Still others said that it wasn't a monster at all, that it must be some sort of giant salamander or lizard and that there might be more of them living in the depths in and around the region. It wasn't a comforting thought.

Yet, no one had any concrete evidence or proof. Yes, there had been the bizarre tracks on the beach, and the sea monster had attacked those poor people on the boat. But no one had any clear pictures or videos of the creature. No one—not even scientists or biologists—could give a definite answer as to what the monster was.

And despite what everyone had seen that day, despite all the witnesses, there were still many people who didn't believe the stories at all. Many people, without proof or evidence, without clear pictures or videos, thought that the sea monster was something made-up, a myth, a story that people had created. One theory was that the sea monster wasn't real, that it was only someone in a costume. This theory was based on the idea that it would be good publicity to bring notoriety to the town, to attract attention and draw visitors to the community. I didn't think that made a lot of sense. Who would want to visit a city if there was a horrible sea monster lurking in the lakes or rivers?

Whatever the reason, the creature was the most popular story for a couple of days. You couldn't go anywhere without hearing someone talking about the sea monster or seeing a picture on television or hearing about it on the radio.

But after a few weeks had passed, and there were no more sightings of the sea monster, the stories faded. It wasn't in the news anymore, and few people talked about it. For a while, people had been warned to be on the lookout if they ventured near any waterways. Many people decided not to go near the water at all.

But as the days passed with no more sightings of the strange sea creature, people gradually began returning to the parks and beaches, to the rivers and lakes. They returned to the water. No one wanted to miss out on summer fun, being that it was such a short season and the time of year when everyone took vacations.

And so, everything slowly returned to normal, until the day things took a turn for the worst . . . for everyone.

19

Two weeks had passed since the sighting of the sea monster, since the people in the boat had been attacked. There had been no more incidents, no more appearances of the strange creature or the mysterious tracks.

"Do you want to go kayaking?" Zach asked me one afternoon. We'd met at my house and were riding our bikes through some nearby trails. He stopped his bike at a sharp turn in the trail, and I stopped next to him.

"I don't know," I said.

"Is it because of that thing?" Zach asked.

"Yeah," I said flatly, adjusting my bike helmet. It had been slipping down my forehead, and I tightened the strap beneath my chin. "I'm not sure it's a good idea."

"You heard what the scientists said," Zach said confidently. "They think it's gone. They're sure the thing has moved into deeper water, and they said there's a good chance we'll never see it again, whatever it was. And that's another thing: they think that it's just some sort of amphibian. You know: some sort of large salamander or mud puppy. It's probably harmless and won't hurt anyone."

I frowned. "Tell that to those people who were in the sailboat," I replied.

"Those people weren't hurt," Zach said. "And besides: they said they never got a good look at the creature, anyway. They jumped off the boat before the thing attacked."

I had to admit that Zach was right. Most likely, we'd seen the last of the creature. Like many animals, the creature—whatever it was—probably just wanted to be left alone. It probably wanted to stay away from people, as it probably sensed them as dangerous. Most wild animals want nothing to do with humans and will try to stay out of their way, hidden from view.

I thought about Zach's suggestion, about going kayaking. It really was a lot of fun.

"I would love to go," I said. "But I don't want to go back to Sherman Park. Is there anywhere else we can kayak?"

"Sure," Zach replied. "There's a place east of the city where there's a park and some boat launches. Maybe we can get my uncle or my mom to haul the kayaks over there. It's only five minutes away, anyway."

So, less than twenty-four hours later, Zach and I were once again paddling his uncle's kayaks through the wide St. Mary's River, the late morning sunshine warming the bare skin of our arms, legs, and faces. This time, however, we were southeast of the city, far from where we'd spotted the sea monster at Sherman Park. My phone was secured within its waterproof case and strapped to my upper-left arm, and I'd already used it a couple of times to take pictures. Unfortunately, I was going to have to limit the amount of time I used my phone. I'd forgotten to put it on the charger overnight, and there was only about ten percent battery life left.

And I will admit that I was more than a little wary, especially when we paddled into deeper water, and I could no longer see the bottom.

"Just think," Zach said with a mischievous grin. "That thing could be anywhere down there, right now, waiting for his chance to—"

"Stop it!" I said, and I slammed the left blade of the double paddle onto the surface, sending a wet spray of water across Zach's back and shoulders. He cringed as the cool water soaked his life vest, T-shirt, and skin.

"Ah!" he hissed. Then smiled. "Actually," he said, "that felt kind of good. We should go for a swim when we get back on land."

"Sounds good," I said. "Let's head back."

We turned our kayaks and began paddling toward shore when my phone rang.

"That's gotta be the goofiest ring tone I've ever heard," Zach said.

I turned my arm and squinted to see the caller ID. "It's my mom," I said, and I rested the paddle on my lap so I could answer.

But I didn't get the chance. I caught a blur of movement in the water near my kayak, and before I could do anything, the sea monster exploded to the surface, upending my kayak and knocking me backward, sending me flying into the air and tumbling into the water.

20

Sometimes, things happen so fast that all you can do is wonder just how they happened. It's as if you don't even have time to worry or panic or be scared, as though you were suddenly propelled into a new reality, like waking up from a bad dream to find yourself in bed. All you can do is gather your senses and move on from where you are.

That's exactly how I felt, because that's exactly what happened. In the blink of an eye, I went from sitting in the kayak to being submerged underwater.

The kayak fell over me, upside down. My buoyant life vest pulled me back to the surface, where I bumped my head on the hard plastic of the kayak.

But fear can do funny things to you. When things happen—scary things, like monsters attacking out of nowhere—adrenalin surges through your body. You find strength you never knew you had, and you can do things you never thought possible.

I flailed about and clambered aboard the overturned kayak. It was awkward, because the narrow vessel kept rolling from side to side, unbalanced. But it was the quickest way to get out of the water. Even so, I wasn't able to climb completely onto the kayak. I held onto it with my arms, gripping the hard shell with every ounce of strength I could manage.

All the while, my phone continued to warble, singing that crazy ring tone I'd programmed.

"Brittany!" Zach yelled from behind me.

I turned my head to see that Zach, too, had been tossed from his kayak. He was now bobbing in the water with one arm over the stern of the vessel, trying to pull himself up.

"Hurry!" I screamed. *"Get out of the water, or that thing is going to get you!"*

Zach wrapped his arms across the kayak and worked to pull himself up. In the meantime, my eyes darted from side to side, up and down, scanning the water around me, searching for any sign of the beast that had upended my kayak, waiting for him to appear again, to grab my legs and pull me under and drag me to his lair in the dark depths.

My attention was diverted by a horn, and I looked up to see a glistening, white boat coming our way. At the bow was a man leaning against a silver railing. He was wearing a cap, sunglasses, white shorts, and a blue shirt. Beside him was a woman with white shorts, a blue blouse, and dark sunglasses. One hand was raised, shading her eyes from the bright sun. Both the man and the woman looked very worried.

They see us! I thought. *They see us, and they're coming to help!*

"Brittany!" Zach hollered. "Are you okay?"

"For now!" I shouted. "But that thing has to be close by!"

The boat horn blared again, indicating that our rescuers were coming. The man in the boat had seen us, and I hoped he would make it in time.

Zach was able to climb back into his kayak, but I remained atop mine. It was upside down, and to get back inside would require me to get back into the water, flip it over, and then climb in. There was no way I was doing that!

"Hey!" a man's voice shouted. I looked up to see the large boat bearing down on us, slowing as it made its final approach. A red and white life ring with a white nylon line attached slapped the water next to me.

I let go of the kayak and grabbed the ring with both arms. Then, I was being pulled, dragged through the water until I reached the boat, where two pairs of arms were waiting. Effortlessly, the man and woman snapped me up and pulled me from the water and onto the boat. I fell to the deck, gasping and heaving, water puddling around me. My breathing was deep and forced.

"Take it easy," the woman said, placing her hand gently on my shoulder. "You're okay. You're okay now."

I coughed and nodded, but I couldn't speak. All I could do was breathe, at least for the moment.

And I thought:

I'm safe. I'm out of the water, in the boat, away from the horrible sea monster that had flipped my kayak and pulled me under. That thing—whatever it was— couldn't get at me.

Zach, however, was still in the water . . . and he wasn't going to be so lucky.

21

"Are you okay?" the man asked. He was standing next to the railing, while the woman knelt next to me on the deck.

Finally, after a couple of more hacks and gasps, I was able to speak. "I'm fine," I choked. "But Zach is still out there!"

"We've got him," the woman said. The man had already tossed the life ring to Zach, who'd grabbed it. Another man emerged from the cabin of the boat, and the two of them began pulling the line. Because Zach was still in his kayak, this action brought both Zach and the small vessel toward the larger boat.

"We'll pull you up!" one of the men shouted. "Leave the kayak for now. We can pick them up when—"

The water around Zach erupted. It was as though a bomb went off directly around him. A shower of foam and white spray rose and swallowed Zach and his kayak.

"Zach!" I wailed.

Even the two men were shocked, and the woman's grip tightened on my shoulder as she shrieked in surprise.

"Zach!" I screamed again.

Instantly, the kayak, as buoyant as it was, popped to the surface and came to rest upside down. Zach popped up next to it, sputtering and gasping, buoyed by his life vest. His eyes were wide and panicky.

"Grab the ring!" one of the men shouted. "Grab it and hang on! We'll pull you up!"

Zach snared the red and white life ring with one arm, pulled it to him, and then grabbed it with the other. He held tightly as both men grasped the line and began hauling, hand over hand, fist over fist.

Behind Zach, water boiled . . . and a head broke the surface.

The sea monster.

For a moment, everything seemed to freeze. Time stopped. Impossible, I know, but that's what it seemed like. That single moment—a sliver in time, a snapshot of horror—is a sight that burned into my brain. It's something that's etched permanently into my memory, something I'll never forget.

He was looking at *me*. I *knew* he was. When the sea monster broke the surface, his piercing eyes connected with mine. And if his eyes could speak, if they conveyed a single message, it was this:

You're next.

No, I thought.

Yes, you. I missed you this time. But not again. Next time . . . .

And then, the monster head vanished. Zach

was being pulled from the water and into the boat, where he collapsed on the deck.

"Are you all right?!?!" the man in the blue shirt asked as he knelt next to my friend.

Zach, coughing and gagging, managed to nod. He tried to speak, but instead only choked out a few garbled words that I couldn't understand.

"Did you see that thing?" I asked.

"Oh, yeah," the man with the blue shirt said, nodding. "We all saw it. So did a *lot* of people."

I frowned and must have looked confused, and the man continued.

"We aren't the only ones who saw it," he said. "Reports are coming in from several places around the river and the canal. People have spotted them in different areas."

Them?

Zach and I looked at one another.

"What do you mean?" I asked. "Do you mean there's . . . there's more than one?"

Again, the man in the blue shirt nodded. The other man had vanished, and the boat's motor roared. The vessel took off with such a jolt that it snapped my head back, and even though I was still seated on the deck, I had to grab the railing to hang on.

"We don't know how many there are," the woman said loudly as the boat picked up speed and churned through the small waves. "All we know is that we need to get to shore. We'll take you to Kemp Marina."

More than one sea monster? I thought. I looked at Zach, and I knew he was thinking the same thing.

More than one?

How many?

Three? Five? Six? A dozen?

A hundred?

It had never occurred to me that there could be more than one.

How many?

How many?

My mind was spinning with questions, but no answers. However, there was one thing I knew for sure: the nightmare for us, and for many people in Sault Ste. Marie, was just beginning.

22

"Where do you live?" the woman asked as the boat plowed through the water. She had helped me to a seat at the stern of the boat, behind the cabin, and was sitting next to me. Zach was sitting on the deck, holding onto the railing. The engine was loud, and we were moving very fast, skimming across the surface, flying across the river as we headed toward shore.

Zach hiked his thumb over his shoulder. "I live over on West 5th Street, not far from Sherman Park," he said.

"And I live on Chestnut Street," I replied.

The woman nodded toward the phone strapped to my arm, still in its protective case. "Can you call your parents to let them know you're okay? Have them come and pick you up at Kemp Marina."

I tried. Unfortunately, by then my phone battery was completely dead. There wasn't enough juice for it to power up.

"The battery's dead," I said, after trying a couple of times.

"You can use mine," the woman said. She stood, went into the cabin for a moment, and returned with her phone. She handed it to me, and I dialed Mom's number, but after several rings, it went to voicemail. I left her a short message telling her that we were okay, that we were going to Kemp Marina, and that my phone was dead and she could call me back at the number I dialed from.

"Not there?" Zach asked when I'd finished leaving a message.

I shook my head. "She might be," I replied.

"But Mom doesn't answer calls from numbers she doesn't recognize."

"Let me try," Zach said, and I handed him the woman's phone. He called his mom but had to leave a message, just like me.

Zach handed the phone back to the woman. "Don't worry," the woman assured us. "You're safe now. We'll be at the marina soon."

The boat skimmed across the surface, leaping over small waves and jostling us about as we held tightly to the thin, metal railing. Meanwhile, the yellow sun burned high in the sky, and the wind played madly with my hair. I saw large and small boats and vessels in the river, and the shore was dotted with homes and structures. Everything looked so peaceful, so normal and inviting. It was hard to believe that a terrible, dark horror was lurking beneath the surface.

Kemp Marina is shaped like a box, surrounded by land with docks on all sides except the entrance. Shaped like it was, it protected the boats from rough weather during a storm. The entrance was big enough for most boats to pass through and dock safely.

As we arrived, the scene was chaos: a mass of bright white confusion as many boats were docking at their slips. Along the docks and in boats, men and women scurried about like beetles. There was anxious talking and distant shouts. Word of the sea monsters had spread and everyone wanted off the water, back to shore, back to land where they would be safe.

Just to the northwest of Kemp Marina is a US Coast Guard Station. A big Coast Guard ship was moored on the other side of the marina, and there were uniformed men and women hurrying about around the marina. Obviously, they had heard about what was happening and had sprung into action. I didn't know what everyone was doing, but they were sure doing it in a big hurry.

To the south of the marina is the enormous Museum Ship Valley Camp, which is a freighter that has been turned into a tourist attraction. You can tour the decks and cargo holds and see what it's like to live and work on a Great Lakes freighter.

As we decelerated to enter the marina, a

slow wave of relief washed over me. I was glad we made it. Yes, we'd had to leave the kayaks behind, but I was sure they would turn up. And even if we lost the kayaks, at least Zach and I were alive. I knew Zach's uncle would understand.

The woman and the two men helped us off the boat and onto the dock. The men secured the boat, and the woman directed her attention to us.

"Is there anyone else you can call?" she asked.

"I can try my dad," I said. "He's at work, and he always has his phone."

Once again, the woman handed over her phone. "Give him a try," she said.

I punched in Dad's number and waited. Meanwhile, as the five of us stood on the dock, we watched the frantic activity going on all around us in Kemp Marina. I was so engrossed in what was happening that I was shocked when I suddenly heard Dad's voice on the phone.

I quickly said, "Hi, Dad."

"Hi, Sweetheart. What's up?"

"Dad!" I said, nearly shouting. "We—I mean

Zach and I—are at Kemp Marina! We saw one of those sea monsters! He attacked us, but we were rescued and you have to—"

"Wait, wait, wait," Dad said, laughing. "Slow down. What's going on?"

I told Dad what had happened, about how we'd been attacked in the river, how the woman and the two men in the boat had saved us, and about the panic all around us at the marina.

"Okay," Dad said. His voice became tense and direct, now that he was aware of the seriousness of the situation. "Don't go anywhere, and I'll pick you guys up in ten minutes."

"Okay," I replied. "See you then."

I handed the phone back to the woman. "My dad is going to pick us up," I told her. "Thanks for letting us use your phone."

"And thanks for saving us," Zach added.

The woman waved it off. "I'm just glad you're safe. I'm glad it's over."

She was, of course, wrong. It wasn't over. Nothing was over, not by a long shot. The *real* horror was only beginning.

23

Zach and I waited in the marina parking lot until we saw Dad's white car pull in. All around, vehicles had been coming and going, people were scurrying about, rushing here and there, carrying bags and totes and coolers from their boats to their cars. Everyone was chatting on their phones; everyone looked worried and frightened.

"You're not going to believe what happened!" I said to Dad as Zach and I climbed into his car. Zach poured into the back, and I climbed into the front.

"Oh, I believe it," Dad said. "At least, I've heard all about it on the radio."

"You have?" Zach asked, fastening his seat belt. I closed the car door and looped the front seat belt over my chest and clicked the buckle into the mechanism, and it made a solid clunk as it latched. My clothing was still soaked, but I didn't care, and Dad didn't notice or simply didn't say anything.

The car began to move again, and Dad glanced into the rearview mirror, then the side mirrors, and then over at me. An earpiece with a small microphone was looped over his ear; he wore it all the time, so he could chat on the phone while driving or working and keep his hands free. He nodded to me.

"It's been all over the news," Dad said. "I'm glad you called. I would have been worried."

That reminded me that my phone was dead. I unhooked the case that was strapped around my arm and removed my phone. I opened up the glove box. A thin, white power cord was coiled like a snake among envelopes, a flashlight, some pens, and a few other odds and ends. I pulled it out and plugged one end into my phone and the other into the port on the dashboard. The phone beeped, alerting me that it was charging.

The car pulled out of the marina, and Zach and I babbled on and on about what had happened. Dad listened, intensely interested, but he seemed a bit in shock, in disbelief.

"But why did that thing come after you?" he asked. "When you were in the kayak?"

I shrugged. "I don't know," I replied. "But that's the second time I've seen him in the river like that."

"The third, actually," Zach chimed in, "if you count the time when we saw the fisherman."

"It's crazy," I said. "This is like—"

Dad's phone chirped. He pressed a button on his earpiece and then raised a hesitant finger in the air. Someone was calling in. I stopped talking.

"Charles Rockensuess," Dad said, very clear and professional-like.

Pause.

Dad looked straight ahead.

His jaw fell.

"That's impossible!" he said.

There was another long pause as he listened. Zach and I, of course, couldn't hear the private conversation.

"Has the leak been stopped?" he asked.

Again, Dad paused and listened.

"I understand," Dad said to the unknown caller. "Yes, yes, of course. I'll be back as soon as I can. I've just got to drop off my daughter and her friend at home, and I'll be right there."

He pressed the button on the earpiece again, terminating the conversation. Then, he let out a long sigh. I couldn't tell if it was a sigh of relief or a sigh of worry and concern.

"That was my office," he said. "We've got an emergency meeting scheduled right away."

"What's going on?" I asked.

"I'm not sure," Dad replied. "But that was our lead product development guy. He says there has been a slow leak at our production facility, and that it might—*might*—somehow be responsible for the sea monsters."

"*What?!?!?*" Zach blurted from the back

seat.

Dad nodded. "I know," he said. "But the theory is that one of our gel products leaked from our factory into the river. It's not toxic, so it's not hurting anything. But the idea is that some of the larger fish have ingested it, and it's created a rapid molecular change in their basic DNA structure."

I turned to look at Zach. He had a puzzled look on his face, and I'm sure I looked equally confused.

"So, what does *that* mean?" I asked.

"It means it's had a highly mutative effect on certain marine life," Dad replied. "In particular, fish. A couple guys in our lab think the result has created an accelerated transformation in the fish, causing them to grow at an incredible rate and create other biological changes."

"Like what?" I asked.

"Well, odd things," Dad replied. "Like growing limbs, the way a tadpole acquires legs to become a frog. It's quite possible that they can move around on land, too. We don't know yet."

"No way," Zach said. "That's crazy."

Dad nodded. "I would agree," he said. "But it's possible. And if it's possible, we have to consider the theory. If it turns out to be true, we've got a big problem on our hands."

Dad wasn't kidding. If what he was saying turned out to be correct, then his company was responsible for creating some of the most horrifying sea monsters in the world.

But that was what they were. *Sea* monsters. Now that we were out of the water, away from the river, we were safe.

Weren't we?

No.

No, we weren't safe.

And Zach and I, along with many other people in Sault Ste. Marie, were about to experience the true meaning of horror.

24

Dad pulled into our driveway. Tires squealed as the car jerked to a quick stop.

"Now, remember what I told you guys," he said. "Get in the house and stay there. Lock the doors and windows."

"But Mr. Rockensuess," Zach said, "we're safe now. Those things are in the water."

"It's only a precaution," Dad told him. "I'm sure you'll be fine; otherwise, I wouldn't leave you here alone. But just to be on the safe side, I want you making sure all the doors and windows are closed and locked. And Brittany, your mom and Bella should be back from Traverse City soon. Don't worry. We'll get all of this straightened out. Just get inside and stay there. Go."

I unplugged the charger from my phone and held it in my hand as I slipped out the car door. My armband had been in my lap, and it fell to the floor. I grabbed the case and opened the door.

Zach opened the rear passenger door and climbed out.

"Remember what I said," Dad said as he leaned forward from the driver's seat. His eyes were narrowed, and he looked very intense and serious. "Get inside the house and don't go anywhere. I'll be home in a while."

I closed the passenger door. While Zach and I hustled to the front of the house, Dad waited in his car, watching.

When we reached the porch, I knelt down. I glanced up at Zach. "Don't tell anyone," I said as I moved a small gray brick that served as a doorstop. Beneath it was a silver key, dulled and soiled by the weather. "We keep this here in case one of us gets accidentally locked out of the house."

Zach grinned. "We have a hidden key, too," he said. "Ours is underneath a flower pot."

I inserted the key into the lock, turned the knob, and pushed the door open. Zach and I scrambled inside and then turned to see Dad in the driveway. Through the windshield, we could see his fist on the dashboard, his thumb hiked in the air, a sign of approval. He turned his head, and his car slowly backed out of the driveway. Then, he raced off.

"I can't believe what he told us," Zach said as we watched Dad's car drive away. "I mean . . . fish turning into sea monsters? That's bizarre."

"But it makes sense," I said. "You heard what Dad said. The fish ate the gel that leaked into the river, and it's turned them into swimming nightmares. Or, at least, that's what the men at Dad's work *think*."

"It's still crazy," Zach said.

"Oh, it's crazy, all right," I agreed. We stepped back, and I began to close the front door.

"But I'm sure they'll get it figured out soon enough, and we'll—"

I felt something against my leg and looked down just in time to see Dora, our cat, slip out the front door.

"Dora! No!" I shouted. I reached down to grab her before she went any further, but it was already too late. Dora bounded across the porch, leapt into the grass, and trotted across the lawn.

"I'll get her," Zach said, and before I could say anything, before I could stop him, Zach was past me and out the door, following in Dora's wake, racing after the cat as she bounced across our neighbor's yard.

"Zach, wait!" I yelled. "Dad said that we should—"

But by then, Zach was already in our neighbor's yard, chasing after the black and white cat. He followed Dora across the next yard and the yard after that, finally sprinting around the side of a house, hot on Dora's trail.

Dora vanished.

Zach disappeared.

The sun bore down from its seat high in an ocean of blue. Swollen, white clouds boiled, swimming in the sky-sea, silent witnesses to the scene below. A blue jay screeched from its perch in a maple tree across the street. From where I stood on the porch, everything seemed calm and peaceful, the perfect summer afternoon.

And then Zach screamed.

Although the day was sunny and hot, a cold chill raced through my body. Zach's scream stunned and shocked me. I tensed, and my skin crawled.

His scream was cut short, sliced in half as though he'd been forced to stop, like someone or something had grasped his throat and squeezed.

Without giving it a second thought, I stuffed my phone into my back pocket and sprang. I jumped off the porch and tore across the front yard, my legs pumping wildly, arms swinging madly, hair flying as I crossed one yard and then the next. I raced to Zach's rescue, wondering what had happened to him, wondering what I would encounter on the other side of the house where I'd watched him vanish only moments before.

"Zach!" I shouted. *"Hang on! I'm on my way!"*

I flew across the green lawns, rounded the corner of the house where Zach and Dora had turned, and stopped . . . completely terrified by what I was now seeing.

A monster.

It was the first time I had been able to get a really good look at one of them. Up until then, I'd caught only short glimpses under water. Even the one that had attacked us earlier that day had appeared only for a moment. Yes, we'd watched that fisherman reel one in from the river bank. But even then, we'd caught only a quick glimpse before we took off, fearing for our lives.

Now, I was able to see one of them up close. And he was *horrible.*

He was a giant monstrosity, a little bit bigger than a normal man. He was covered in large, plate-like scales, dirty green-blue in color. There were a few small chunks of seaweed and gooey algae sticking to him. His arms, which were spread out, were wide and wing-like, and his hands—which were really more like stubby claws than anything else—were webbed. His scaly legs were like tree trunks. He had a tail of sorts, not quite long enough to reach the ground. His back was to me, so I couldn't see his face, but I didn't need nor want to. I already knew the water beast looked *hideous.*

I suddenly remembered the words of my dad in the car.

It's quite possible that they can move around on land, too, he had said. *We don't know yet.*

Now, I knew.

Zach's eyes were wide. He was holding Dora in his arms, backed into a corner of the house, surrounded by knee-high, dark green bushes. The monster was only a few feet away from him, and Zach had nowhere to go. Dora was hissing at the beast and struggling to get out of Zach's grip. I was sure my cat was just as scared as we were, and the poor thing wanted to get away as fast as she could.

Zach looked horrified, too. Backed into the corner like he was, he had nowhere to run, no chance for escape. He was trapped. Still, he held onto Dora tightly, protecting her. If Zach and Dora were going to be saved, it was going to be up to me.

"Hey!" I shouted, surprising myself. I had never really considered myself a very brave person, but here I was, about to face down a terrifying sea monster, attempting to draw its attention away from my friend so he could escape with my cat.

And it worked.

The horrible thing turned, took one look at me, and began walking in my direction. It didn't move all that fast, thankfully, and I was hoping that I would be able to outrun it.

"Now's your chance!" I shouted to Zach. *"Run, while he's not looking at you!"*

As soon as Zach turned and ran, I did the same. And although I had been hoping that the beast wasn't all that fast, it turned out that he was quite agile. He didn't run, but he moved swiftly and decisively, and one glance over my shoulder told me that he might be faster than I was, that I just might not make it back to our house in time.

So, when I rounded our neighbor's house, my eyes darted from side to side, looking for a place to hide. If I can't outrun him, maybe I can outsmart him.

There.

By the porch, next to the house, was a large growth of thick, green cedar bushes, tightly trimmed. I knew I'd only have a split-second to hide before the monster came around the corner and spotted me. If he saw me, or if he saw where I was hiding, then I would be cornered, and I'd be just as helpless as Zach and Dora had been only moments before.

I took one giant, powerful bound and dove headfirst into the bushes. Branches scratched at my bare skin and tore at my clothing, but that was the very least of my worries. I wasn't concerned about a few cuts and scrapes when there was a giant sea monster coming after me!

I curled into a ball, tucking tightly in the

space between the bushes and the house. My heart was pounding so hard that I thought it was going to crack my rib cage. My breath was heaving, and I tried to breathe through my nose so that I wouldn't make so much noise that I'd attract the sea monster.

Through the bushes, I could make out a dark shape. The huge monster had slowed, no doubt confused about where I had gone.

He stopped.

I held my breath.

A bird chirped. Far away, I heard sirens and a car honk twice.

The beast stalked, moving slowly, warily.

Searching.

For me.

And just when I thought it was going to pass me by, just when I thought that I had been able to escape detection, the unthinkable happened.

In my back pocket, my phone rang, singing that crazy ring tone loud and shrill. I knew then that I would be discovered, that there would be no escape.

26

The sound coming from my back pocket was awful. Oh, it wasn't meant to be. I had downloaded the ring tone because I thought it was cute and funny and different.

Now, it was like a wailing alarm that alerted the sea monster to my exact location. The sound would lead him right to me.

I quickly dug my phone from my pocket and glanced at the caller ID.

Mom. Again.

Normally, I would have answered the call. I

think anybody would. If Mom calls, you answer the phone, no matter what.

But this wasn't any normal situation. At the time, I couldn't just sit in the bushes and chat on the phone with Mom, telling her that I was being chased by a horrible sea monster. I wanted badly to talk to her, but it was going to have to wait.

So, I quickly pressed the *reject* button, silencing the ring.

The sea monster had heard the ring. He was moving slowly toward me, approaching cautiously, curiously. I could only hope that he wouldn't see me tucked deeply in the bushes.

Closer . . . .

Please don't see me. Please don't see me. Please don't see me . . . .

Closer . . . .

The bushes moved, and I realized I was only seconds away from being discovered. The beast knew where I was, knew I was there. He knew where I was hiding.

I couldn't just sit there and allow myself to become lunch. I knew that if I waited any longer, it would be too late. I'd be trapped between the monster and the house. There would be nowhere to run. I had to act, I had to move, to make an attempt to get away in the last second that I had.

Still gripping my phone, I sprang sideways, crawling on my hands and knees along the narrow space between the bushes and the house. Once again, sharp branches poked and prodded at me. A dry, sticky spider web stuck to my face, and I quickly wiped it away.

Finally, I broke free from the bushes and ran. However, instead of heading directly home, I turned left and sprinted along the side of the house, through the back yard next to a large, above-ground pool.

I turned.

The sea monster was coming.

I continued running, turning to loop around close to the pool, hoping I could keep my distance and make it to the front of the house, and then home.

The sea monster kept coming, and he was gaining, closing the distance between us.

Suddenly, my phone rang again, and before I even looked at the caller ID, I knew that Mom was calling again. I hadn't answered her first call, and I'm sure she'd become worried and called again. I knew she'd continue to call and call until I answered the phone.

Still running, I snapped my arm up to press the *answer* button . . . but the phone slipped. It slipped and fell out of my hand, and at the worst possible time. The phone, still chirping loudly, flew through the air, where it landed with a loud *plop!* into the above-ground pool. Even as it sank to the bottom, I could hear it ringing, although fainter and muffled through the water.

And although my phone was still in its waterproof case, I certainly couldn't stop to retrieve it! My only hope would be to make it home safely and return later to get my phone from the bottom of the pool.

So, I kept running. When I reached the house, I turned, snapping my head around to see where the creature was.

When I saw him, I slowed to a stop. My

chest was heaving, my breathing was forced, and my heart hammered.

The sea monster was no longer chasing me. He'd stopped next to the pool, leaning over the side, staring curiously into the water.

What is he doing? I wondered.

It took me a moment to realize that his attention had been caught by the ringing of my phone. Although I couldn't hear it from where I was, I was certain the sea monster could hear it. It seemed he'd completely forgotten about me and was now focused on the phone, which was now resting at the bottom of the pool, still ringing.

And if that were the case, if the monster was distracted by the phone, that would mean I would only have a few moments before the ringing stopped. How long would the creature stand by the edge of the pool, listening?

I wasn't going to find out. While he was distracted, I had to get away. It was the break I needed, and I intended to use it.

I turned and ran, not looking back. When I reached the front of the house, I turned again, heading in the direction of our home only a few yards away. I saw Zach, still running, still carrying Dora in his arms. He'd made it to our driveway. He was safe.

I ran and ran, not stopping until I'd reached our yard. Zach had stopped at the porch and turned, facing me. Dora was in his arms. The cat didn't look the least bit frightened. In fact, she looked as if this was just a normal day for her.

"You made it!" Zach shouted.

I stopped at the porch, my breathing hard and heavy.

"Just barely," I gasped. "Come on! Let's get inside!"

We went into the house. I slammed the front door closed and locked it. Then, I leaned my back against the door and slid down until I was sitting on the floor.

Zach placed Dora on the couch, and the cat bounded away as though nothing out of the ordinary had happened. Zach sat on the footstool. He leaned forward and placed his face in his hands.

We were safe in our house. For how long, I didn't know. But we'd made it. We'd be safe for the time being.

Zach raised his head and looked at me. "How did you get away?" he asked.

"I was running by my neighbor's pool," I replied, "and my phone started ringing. When I tried to answer it, it slipped out of my hands and into the water. It was still ringing in the water, and the—"

I stopped speaking and didn't finish my sentence. My mind had suddenly been snared by a different idea altogether.

It was a crazy idea, I know. But if it worked, we just might be able to capture the sea monsters.

27

In the kitchen, we have a cordless phone hanging from the wall next to the refrigerator. I raced to it and plucked it from the charging receptacle.

"What?" Zach asked as I leapt to my feet to grab the phone. Lines formed on his forehead as he furrowed his brow. "What are you thinking?"

"Hang on," I said. "I'm calling Dad."

Dad answered on the second ring.

"Dad!" I said. "I think I know a way we can catch the sea monsters!"

I explained to Dad how nearly every time

we'd spotted the sea monster, my phone had been ringing. The only other time was when the fisherman in the river near Mission Creek had hooked it. To me, it was too much of a coincidence. It was as though the monsters had been attracted to the sound of my phone's ring tone. I told him about the most recent episode, how the monster was distracted by my phone when I accidentally dropped it into the pool. I explained that if the sea monsters were attracted by the ring tone, maybe that same sound could be used to lure them to some sort of trap where they could be captured.

"Think about it," I said. "If phones with waterproof cases were placed in a certain area of the river, the sea monsters would be attracted to them. All of the phones would have to have the same ring tone, of course. But maybe the sound would lure them all into one area."

Dad listened quietly, without saying anything. He was so silent that I thought perhaps the call had been dropped.

"Dad?" I said. "Are you still there?"

"I'm here, Brittany," he said. "I'm just thinking. You might be right. Sound can travel far under water. If the phone and that crazy ring are beneath the surface, it just might attract the sea monsters."

Dad told me to stay indoors, that he would be home soon. He said he'd also talked to Mom and that she and Bella were on their way back from Traverse City. Dad said Mom had been worried when I hadn't answered the phone. He said he didn't have time to explain everything to her, but told her that I was safe at home and that Zach was with me.

I returned the phone to the charger on the wall and turned to see Zach. While talking to my dad, I'd nearly forgotten my friend, leaning against the counter.

"Did you catch all that?" I asked.

Zach nodded. "I did, and I think it's brilliant. What's your dad going to do?"

I shook my head. "I don't know. But he said he'd be home soon."

"That was great thinking on your part," Zach

said. "It never occurred to me that the only time we saw the sea monster was when your phone was ringing. Except for when the fisherman had snagged that one in the canal."

"Well," I said, "I could be wrong. But you should have seen the way that thing looked at my phone in the pool. He was completely focused on it. It *must* have been the ring tone that held his attention."

Zach used my phone to call his mom. She didn't answer, and he left a message simply saying that he was with me at my house and that we were okay.

Ten minutes later, we heard a car skid to a halt in the driveway. I was sure it was Dad, and it was. As I stood, the front door of our house burst open. Dad stood in the doorway, holding the knob with one hand, leaning forward.

"Come with me," he said, gesturing with his free hand. "We're heading back to Kemp Marina. I'll explain on the way."

Zach and I took a quick glance at one another, and then we were on our way. We hustled into Dad's waiting car in the driveway and sped off. Before we headed to the marina, Dad stopped at the house where I'd dropped my phone, and we retrieved it from the pool. Thankfully, we were able to get it using the pool skimmer, so none of us had to jump into the pool.

Then, while we drove, Dad told me what had happened in the short time since we'd spoken on the phone. He told me that he'd called the Coast Guard, and they had liked my idea. They said there was a chance it might work, but they would need the right ring tone, the same one that I'd used on my phone.

That meant I needed to show them what one it was, where I'd downloaded it. That's why Dad had stopped to get my phone before heading to the marina.

I listened as Dad explained all this and found myself in a sort of dazed disbelief. Usually when someone my age comes up with some sort of plan like this, they aren't taken seriously by grown-ups. Adults think boys and girls my age are fine and all that, but we're just not old enough, smart

155

enough, or wise enough to come up with what could be considered a grown-up, thoughtful, responsible solution to a serious problem. And most of the time, maybe adults are right. Most kids my age don't have the experience that adults have when it comes to solving and dealing with real-world issues, especially when people's lives were at stake.

Like now.

But now, my plan was going to be put into action. My plan was going to be used to capture the sea monsters. If it worked, I might even be a hero.

But if it failed, it would mean disaster. Maybe worse.

I would be responsible for that, too.

The thought terrified me as the car raced toward the marina, toward a new horror that I could never have imagined.

28

I'd expected the marina to be a swarm of frantic activity, with people rushing here and there. I thought there might be police cars with lights and sirens blaring, with men and women in uniforms with guns and tools strapped to thick belts around their waists, looking all important and official.

But that's not the way it was at all.

In fact, the marina looked bare and desolate. Most of the cars in the parking lot were gone. There were many boats docked in their slips, of course, but there wasn't a single person in sight.

Everyone had fled the marina, either on orders of the Coast Guard or simply out of fear. No one wanted to be near the water where strange, giant beasts lurked in the depths.

At the entrance of the marina parking lot, two uniformed Coast Guardsmen each raised a hand, indicating we should stop. Dad rolled down his window and explained who he was. After a quick glance at Zach in the backseat and me in the front, they waved us through. We parked quickly and scrambled out of the car.

It was then that I saw how busy things really were. From the far side of the parking lot, we really couldn't see much of what was going on in the marina. Now that we were closer, we could see that a lot was happening. Several uniformed men and women walked along the docks, staring down into the water. Some pointed, some gazed out far into the river.

A uniformed man emerged from a building and hustled toward us. He introduced himself to my dad, and the two men talked. As we listened, we learned that Dad had already been speaking to this man on the phone, telling him about my suspicion regarding the ring tone, how there was a good possibility that my phone's ring tone could attract the monster.

"I don't know what's different about the ring tone on your daughter's phone," the man said. "After we spoke on the phone, we tried using a regular ring tone, and that didn't seem to work. We tried some other sounds, too, but that didn't seem to attract the creatures, either. So, I don't know what's so different about the ring tone on your daughter's phone that will make any difference, but we're willing to give it a try."

Dad turned and nodded at me. "We can use her phone," he said. "It's got a waterproof case."

The uniformed man nodded. "I don't think we'll need her phone," he said. "Just the ring tone. We've got our own phones to use, and they have waterproof cases, too."

"I think I can send a copy of the ring tone to your phone," I said. "You should be able to send it to all the other phones you want to use."

"That's a good idea," the man said. "Instead

of using it as a ring tone, we can build a sound file and play an endless loop."

I hadn't thought of that. That would make it much easier than trying to call all the phone numbers to make the phones ring.

"We're going to attach the phones to lines and lower them into the water around the marina," the man said. "Like I said: we've already tried using some other sounds, but we haven't had much luck. I'm really hoping that your ring tone —whatever it is—will work."

"But what if we're too far away?" Zach asked. "What if the sea monsters don't hear the ringing?"

"Oh, I think they'll hear it," the man said. "Sound can travel great distances under water, and most marine life have very acute hearing. Anything within a few miles of the ringing will hear it, I'm sure."

It took about twenty minutes to get everything ready. Sharing my ring tone was easy enough, as all I needed to do was send it to the man's phone number.

After that, my work was pretty much done. Zach and I spent most of our time keeping out of the way of the busy men and women who were making preparations. They brought in a long, large net to string up across the front of the marina. The net was affixed with weights so it sank, which would allow the sea monsters to swim into the marina. When a signal was given, men and women on either side of the entrance would pull on the net, which would cause the top portion to rise to the surface and create a barrier, trapping the sea monsters in the marina.

Or, at least, that was the idea.

There wasn't much for Zach and me to do, so we just hung out at the dock near the shore, watching everyone else work. I would have liked to have been part of the action, doing something to help out, but there really wasn't a lot two kids would be able to help with.

And really, after thinking about it, there really wasn't a reason for Zach and me to be there. I could have sent the ring tone from our house to anyone, so it really wasn't necessary for us to be at the marina.

But I was glad I was there and not at home. It was kind of exciting just being there, watching the action, feeling the excitement and anticipation. Things were happening; there was electricity in the air. And danger. And suspense. It was kind of fun, being so close to the action.

Not far away in the marina parking lot, a television news crew had arrived. They'd parked a van and set up equipment, and a woman was holding a microphone, facing a man who was holding a large camera on his shoulder. Exciting things were going on, and I liked being so close to all the action.

And then, farther out along the docks, we heard a piercing scream—and a splash.

29

The noise made everyone in the marina stop what they were doing. For a split instant, the only thing that could be heard were a few gulls screeching as they cartwheeled over the warm breeze above the marina.

Then, there were the sounds of footsteps and shouts and intense activity as everyone sprang to action.

"Is it a sea monster?!?" I asked Zach.

"I don't know," Zach replied. "I hope not. I don't think anyone is ready for it just yet. They haven't even put the phones in the water."

To our relief, we soon found out that a man had simply slipped off the dock. He'd lost his footing and tumbled into the water, but was safely pulled out by several other people. Thankfully, he hadn't been hurt.

Dad had been away for a few minutes, and now we saw him hurrying toward us. The television crew tried to flag him down for an interview, but he waved them off, shaking his head, saying that he was sorry, but he just didn't have time at the moment.

"I think we're about ready," he told us. "They've got your ring tone on all the phones. Each one will play an endless loop, over and over. It might take some time, especially if the creatures are a ways away. But if they show up, we'll be ready."

It sounded like a good plan, and I felt a little proud of myself. After all, it had been my idea in the first place.

And it seemed with the help of so many men and women, so many people, that the plan couldn't possibly fail. I thought the worst thing that could happen would be that the monsters didn't hear the ring tone or for some reason didn't show up.

Of course, I shouldn't have worried. My plan was going to work even better than I had imagined. The sea monsters were about to show up . . . but things were about to go terribly, terribly wrong.

30

We were taken inside a building to wait in a room that overlooked the water. It was some sort of office, with a desk and several filing cabinets. There were nautical paintings and pictures on the wall and a big window that faced the harbor. From where Zach and I were, we had a clear view of the marina and all of the boats moored within.

There was a radio on the desk, and it squawked every couple of minutes. Men and women were barking orders, confirming procedures, reporting on the status of things at particular locations around the marina. Through the window, we could see whirling drones in the air, hovering above the docks like buzzing, mechanical dragonflies, slowly moving back and forth in zigzag patterns over the harbor.

Five minutes went by. Then ten. Then thirty. An hour passed. Dad came to check on us once; he was with a few of the Coast Guardsmen, as well as a few other men from his work.

"How are you guys doing in here?" he asked.

"Pretty bored," I said.

"Well, there's nothing new to report out there," he said. "So far, there's been no sign of anything."

"Maybe I was wrong," I said sheepishly. "Maybe that thing wasn't attracted by the ring tone, after all."

"We'll give it some more time," Dad said, glancing at his watch. "The day's not over yet. And besides: if any of those things are far away, it will take them some time to get here."

Dad left. Zach and I were alone in the room.

"I'll bet your dad is right," Zach said. "It's

just taking some time. Maybe those things hear the sound, but it's taking them time to swim to the marina."

"Maybe," I said, but I wasn't that hopeful. "I thought that if the sea monsters were going to show up, they would have been here by now."

Tick—

Time dragged.

—tock . . . .

The radio spluttered with tinny voices, nothing new to report.

Tick—

The drones hung lazily in the air, moving in their insect patterns, crossing back and forth across the marina.

—tock . . . .

Zach spoke. "I wonder if—"

His sentence was cut off by a man's urgent voice on the radio.

"Okay, okay, we've got a big shadow moving beneath the surface! Northeast corner of the marina! Moving south, toward the docks!"

Zach and I dashed to the window, pressing

our noses against the glass. Of course, there was nothing to see except the white boats shining in the sun and the blue sky above. Two drones broke their routine pattern and slowly moved to the mouth of the marina.

"He's inside the harbor," the voice came again. "Probably five or six feet under the surface. Moving fast. Let's raise the net and close off the marina. That'll trap him."

"Negative," another voice replied. "Let's wait until he gets farther in."

Several people came into view, rushing along the docks. Dad was one of them, along with a few people from his work. They walked swiftly, heads down, their eyes scanning the water.

"Okay," the voice on the radio said. "It looks like he's stopped near one of the phones in the water. All I can see is a dark shadow beneath the surface."

The excitement I felt was like electricity running through my blood. Yes, I'll admit I was a bit scared, but the exhilaration I felt was boiling. On one hand, I wanted to stay in the office where it was safe; on the other hand, I wanted to be out on the docks, closer to the action where I could see what was going on in the water and around the marina.

A group of men had stopped walking and were peering down into the water, but from where we were, we couldn't see what they were looking at. One man held a camera, and he was pointing it at the water. Two men held phones to their ears. Above the group, a white drone hung, suspended in the air, glowing white in the blazing sun, blades whirring like the wings of a hummingbird.

The radio in our room crackled.

"Okay, hang on, hang on," the man's voice said. He sounded excited, urgent. "We've got *another* thing moving, coming into the marina, below the surface! And there's *another* one! One more! Now there's *four* of them!"

My heart hammered. *Four?* I thought. *How many are there?*

And then, near the docks, the water exploded upward, a blooming flower of dark water and foam. An enormous sea monster, hideous and ugly and terrible, flung himself partially onto the dock. The small crowd splintered as the men ducked and dove to get away . . . but not all of them were going to make it. Two of the men—including my dad—were dragged off the dock and down into the water, helpless, in the clutches of a horrible water beast.

31

Without any consideration of the consequences, and without really knowing if there was anything I could do, I turned, bolted to the door, flung it open, and burst into the harsh sunlight. I was dimly aware of Zach saying something behind me, but I don't remember what it was.

The only thing I knew was that thing had grabbed my dad and pulled him off the dock, and I couldn't stand in a room several dozen feet away and not do anything to help.

But at least I wasn't alone. Several other

people had sprung to assist. A uniformed woman grabbed a nearby red and white life ring and tossed it into the water. Another man had bravely leapt into the water himself, and he vanished beneath the surface with a heavy splash. There was lots of shouting and yelling, lots of orders barked. Somewhere, a siren screamed, and I was also aware of the thudding *whopwhopwhopwhopwhop* of an approaching helicopter.

"Dad!" I screamed as I reached the place on the dock where he'd been attacked. *"Dad!"*

I stopped at the edge of the dock so abruptly that Zach ran into me. I lost my balance and began to tumble forward, my arms pinwheeling to regain balance. Fortunately, at the very last second, Zach grabbed my upper arm and pulled me back.

Below, in the water, three men thrashed in a turbulent eruption of foamy madness. I saw thrashing arms, whirling legs, and rolling heads. I heard gasps and gurgles and choked grunts.

And the sea monster.

I could catch glimpses of him, too, as he tried to pull the men down into a dark, watery grave. One of the men had succeeded in grasping the life ring, and he clung to it tightly until he was yanked violently beneath the surface.

And my dad.

He was swirling and churning about, kicking and thrashing. Water flew. In the chaos and confusion, I could see the blue-green scales of the sea monster and his hideous face, the claws on his webbed hands and feet, his powerful arms and legs. It was like watching a horror movie—only much, much worse.

I think the most terrible thing of all was knowing there was nothing we could do. Zach and I were two kids—much smaller than adults—and not nearly as strong. We had nothing to defend us, nothing we could use to help the men in the water.

However, more people were rushing to help. People were running, coming toward us. I hoped they would be able to reach Dad and the other men in time, before they were pulled under by the sea monster.

But there was one thing I hadn't thought about, and neither had Zach.

We were standing at the very edge of the dock, looking down into the water at the bizarre scene, at the constant flailing, the spraying water, a twisting, churning battle of arms and legs and gasping men, when the sea monster's leg slammed into one of the dock's support beams. It snapped like a dry twig . . . and in the next moment, before we could get back, before we could leap to safety, Zach and I were sent tumbling down, splashing into the water.

There had been no warning. One moment we were standing at the edge of the dock, and the next we were plunging straight down, our footing yanked from beneath us. There was nothing to grab, no way to save ourselves.

And then we were in the water.

Instantly, I was submerged. Water filled my mouth, but I was able to spit it out before swallowing it. I struggled to the surface, a spluttering, frantic, drenched mess, confused, afraid. Zach and I were a tangled mess of thrashing legs and flailing arms and racing heartbeats and tense muscles, flashing blue sky and lemony sun. I was aware that there were others around me in the water: Zach, my dad, another man—

—*and the sea monster.* Although I couldn't see him or see much of anything else, I was acutely aware that the creature was the reason for our intense struggle. He had pulled my dad and the other men from the dock, and I knew his intention was to pull them beneath the surface. Now, Zach and I faced the very same danger.

Something grabbed my leg and pulled me under again. I opened my mouth to scream, which was a mistake. Water rushed into my mouth and down my throat. My immediate reaction was an involuntary heave to expel the fluid, and I thought I was going to throw up.

Then, my head popped above the surface. I was coughing and gagging, still flailing wildy with my arms, struggling to escape, to get away, to get out of the water before I was yanked under again. Zach was next to me, and he, too, was thrashing and gasping.

Meanwhile, above us, men and women had gathered around the edges of the collapsed deck. I was vaguely aware of shouting and yelling. Then, the red and white life ring suddenly slapped the water next to me, appearing as though it had materialized out of nowhere. I looped my arms around it, and instantly, I was yanked from the water. The ring was slippery, and I didn't have a solid grip. I heard a man's voice telling me to hold on tight, that everything was going to be all right. I was pulled from the water, up, up, toward the edge of the damaged dock, water dripping from my soaked shorts and shirt.

And then many hands were reaching for me, lifting me, pulling me to safety. I don't remember the hands grabbing me or how I got to the deck. I was on my side, soaking wet, coughing, and a hand was on my shoulder. Zach suddenly appeared next to me, laying sideways, choking and spitting water.

Shouting and yelling continued, and suddenly I heard my dad's voice.

"Are you all right?"

I was so shocked and relieved that I rolled to my other side to face his voice. Dad was kneeling next to me, dripping wet, his drenched white shirt torn and ragged. He had a small cut on his forehead that was bleeding a little, but not bad.

"I thought that thing was going to get you!" I said, and I wrapped my arms around him. He hugged me for a moment and then drew back. He searched my eyes.

"I'm fine," he said. "You okay?"

I nodded.

Dad looked at Zach. "How about you?"

"Yeah," Zach said. "I'm fine, now that I'm out of the water."

"You guys hang tight," Dad said. "I've got to help out. I think we've got these things corralled, if we can keep them in the marina, in the water. Go back into that office, and stay there. Don't go anywhere. You'll be safe there. You understand?"

Zach and I nodded. Dad got up and hustled off, and once again, we were left alone while the marina was teeming with activity.

"Well," Zach said, wiping his face with his hands. "At least we know your plan worked. The weird ring attracted the sea monsters."

"Maybe a little too well," I said.

"And more than one of them, too," he said.

Suddenly, I didn't want to be at the marina. I wanted to be home, to be anywhere away from the action, away from the chaos and craziness of the marina. I wanted to be safe.

Zach and I stood, and we glanced around the marina. Near the mouth, we could see that the large net had been stretched across the opening and was set in place, spanning a wide area and closing off the marina from the river. Nothing in the water would be able to escape, except smaller fish that could slip through the net.

How anyone intended to capture the sea monsters was anybody's guess. Now that they were trapped within Kemp Marina, what would happen next? What would happen to them?

But that wasn't something I was going to worry about. I was worried about Dad, of course, but now that he was out of the water, he was out of danger. Now that the giant net was secured, now that the creatures had been trapped within the confines of the small harbor, most of the danger was over.

And I was really, really glad.

From the office window, we watched and waited for nearly two hours. There were a few exciting moments when we saw the sea creatures lifted from the water in big nets, but the beasts appeared still and lifeless. I thought they were dead. Later, we found that they'd been shot with some sort of tranquilizing drug that made them go to sleep. The creatures—four of them in all—were loaded into a large, white box truck and hauled away for studying.

Meanwhile, the television news crew was

busy filming and reporting. As you can imagine, the story was a huge sensation. I was hoping that Zach and I would be interviewed, but that didn't happen. Instead, they interviewed my dad and a few people from his work. They also interviewed some of the emergency responders like the police and Coast Guard. That evening after dinner, Mom, Dad, and I watched the television news. It was cool to see the story on TV, knowing that Zach and I had been there, that we had watched everything happen with our own eyes.

Less than a week later, there was a follow-up story. All of the sea monsters had been taken to a special pool at a nearby college. The pool had been drained of its water because they needed to eliminate the added chemicals like chlorine, as they knew it would probably kill the creatures. Then, they'd built a special fence around the pool so the creatures wouldn't be able to get out and refilled it with fresh water.

However, after a day or so, the sea monsters had returned to their original state and became fish once again! Scientists discovered that the creatures were, as suspected, fish that had been eating the accidental discharge from the factory, and the effect simply wore off after a while. The scientists were left with only four large fish swimming around in the large pool.

Of course, that didn't mean the creatures had been harmless. Scientists and experts speculated that the sea monsters could have been very dangerous while they were wild in and around Sault Ste. Marie and the St. Mary's River. They said that it was incredible that no one had been seriously hurt.

Still, many people had been freaked out by what had happened, and it took a few weeks for things to get back to normal. Many people were still worried about the sea monsters, thinking that there might be more that hadn't been captured.

But gradually, as the summer plodded along and the memory of the horrible sea monsters began to fade, people began returning to the beaches and the parks.

And we even got the kayaks back! They had washed ashore not far from where we'd had to leave them in the river, and a homeowner had found them and called the police to report it. Zach's mom saw a picture of them in a lost-and-found section of the newspaper and recognized them as belonging to her brother, who is, of course, Zach's uncle. Zach and I were super-glad about that, because we both felt bad about losing the kayaks. We were happy that someone had found them and turned them in.

July gave way to August. Stores began stocking back-to-school items, a reminder that the warm, sunny days would be coming to an end, giving way to cooler days and even colder nights. Winter would follow, with its white fury of snow and ice and howling arctic winds.

I was excited about the beginning of school, and on the first day, I was thrilled to find out that Zach was in my class. It was a new school for me, with new people and teachers, and I was glad to have a friend who made me feel comfortable. Zach knew a lot of people, and he seemed very well-liked by his classmates.

But there was another new kid, who, like me, had moved to Sault Ste. Marie over the summer. He was quiet and shy, and he never looked at anyone. I thought he might be lonely, so when I saw him sitting by himself one day in the lunchroom, I went over to talk to him. I sat on the bench opposite him, and just as I was introducing myself, Zach saw me. He came over with his tray and sat down, too.

"Hi," I said.

"Hey," the boy replied.

"How's it going?" Zach said.

The boy shrugged. "Okay, I guess."

His name was Jackson Porter. He didn't talk much, so Zach and I did most of the speaking while trying to include the new boy. He seemed distant and distracted, maybe a little nervous, but his interest was awakened when Zach and I recounted what had happened over the summer with the sea monsters.

"I heard about that," the boy said, suddenly becoming alert and aware. "It was on the news. But it's nothing like—"

He stopped himself and looked away quickly, and I got the impression that he didn't want to say anything more.

Zach and I looked at each other, and our thoughts connected. We both knew that the new kid was bothered by something.

"Like what?" Zach asked.

"Never mind," Jackson replied. "It's too crazy, anyway."

"Hey," I said. "We thought sea monsters were crazy. But it really happened."

"I think what happened to me and my friend was a lot worse than monsters in the water," Jackson said.

"What could be worse than *that?*" Zach asked. He'd finished most of his lunch and was now scooping up a spoonful of what appeared to be chocolate pudding.

"Dogman," Jackson replied. His voice was

hushed and soft, and he didn't look at us when he spoke.

Again, Zach and I looked at each other.

"What?" I asked. I'd heard what he said, but I didn't know what he was talking about.

However, Zach's eyes grew. "I've heard of the Michigan Dogman," he said. "The legend goes back a long time."

"He's not a legend," Jackson said, shaking his head. He looked at me and then at Zach. His eyes were focused, serious. "He's real. I know."

"Really?" Zach said.

Jackson nodded his head. "Yep," Jackson replied. "It happened last year on Drummond Island. My friend Delaney and I almost—"

Jackson stopped speaking, as if he was afraid of sharing a deep, dark secret.

"Who is Delaney?" I asked.

"A friend," Jackson replied. "But there's not enough time right now to explain everything. Meet me at the playground during recess, and I'll tell you what happened. Okay?"

"Okay," I answered, and I glanced at Zach.

"Sure," Zach replied. "See you then."

So, later that afternoon, the three of us—Zach, Jackson, and I—huddled beneath a big oak tree during recess. We all sat, cross-legged, facing each other. Jackson began to speak.

And that's how Zach and I learned a horrifying story—the story of the Drummond Island Dogman.

Next:

Johnathan Rand's

MICHIGAN

CHILLERS®

#19: Drummond Island Dogman

Continue on for a FREE preview!

1

The sky was gray and the clouds held rain.

"Jackson, are you sure you know where you're going?" Delaney asked loudly. She was seated beside me on the side-by-side off-road vehicle, and had to shout over the roaring engine. On top of that, we were both wearing helmets that covered our ears, which made communication difficult.

"I told you," I said. "I know this land like I know my bedroom. My dad owns over one hundred acres. I grew up here, hiking and riding all over the place.

There's no way I can get lost."

"I hope not," Delaney said. "It looks like it's going to rain at any second."

"And that'll make it even *more* fun," I said. "The trails get all muddy, and we will, too!"

Delaney Granger and I had set out earlier in the afternoon in my side-by-side, which is sort of a souped-up, four-wheel-drive go kart, designed especially for off-road use. We'd been riding the trails on our property on Drummond Island, Michigan. Drummond Island is, in my opinion, the coolest place anyone could possibly live. I admit that I haven't traveled all over the country, but I've seen and read about some great places. To me, there's no place better than Drummond Island. It's a big island that's part of Michigan's Upper Peninsula. More than two thirds of the island is owned by the State of Michigan, so it's public property. However, there are only about twelve hundred people who live here. Maybe not even *that* many. The island is named after General Sir Gordon Drummond, Governor-General and Administrator of Canada who died way back in 1854.

There's only one school on the island, and there are only about fifty students. I'm in fifth grade.

Delaney is in the same grade, and she's a few months older than me. We met last summer when her family came to the island to help take care of her grandmother. Unfortunately, her grandma passed away over the winter. But Delaney's family loved Drummond so much that they decided to move to the island permanently earlier this spring.

There are only three ways you can get to Drummond Island. There is a small airport, but there aren't any commercial airlines. You can arrive by boat, if you have one. Or, you can come by car, which is what most people do. So, if you ever want to come to the island with a vehicle, you have to take the ferry from De Tour Village. Cars drive onto the flat, barge-like vessel that safely transports them and their occupants across the St. Mary's River. The distance is about a mile, and it doesn't take very long. My Dad and I have been back and forth across the river on the ferry a billion times.

But what I like best about Drummond Island? Animals. There are all sorts of creatures that inhabit the wilds of Drummond Island. Deer, bear, raccoon, squirrels, chipmunks, coyotes, weasels, foxes, rabbits, woodchucks, and all sorts of birds. There are even a few moose on the island. The ponds and lakes have frogs, fish, and turtles of all types and sizes.

There is one other kind of animal—a predator—that inhabits the island, although you'll hardly ever see them. I'm talking, of course, about wolves. I've heard there are only a few on the island, but I've never seen them or their tracks. When I was little, I remember hearing them howling one night, and it freaked me out.

So, I don't worry too much about wolves while I'm hiking in the forest or riding the trails on the side-by-side. I don't worry about bears, because they like to keep to themselves, too. In fact, there aren't any animals on Drummond Island that I'm afraid of.

But that was about to change.

I carefully needled the side-by-side along a thin trail down a hill, maneuvering around tight corners and over deep, jutting ruts. The knobby, wide tires handled most trails and hills with ease. I was taking Delaney to one of my favorite places: a small pond in a low-lying area, deep within the island.

"Here it is," I said, leaning a bit closer to Delaney so she could hear. As we approached the edge of the pond, I shut off the engine. It spluttered twice, then stopped.

"Pretty cool," Delaney said.

"This is where I found Hops," I said, pointing. "He was right over there."

Two summers ago, I found an injured baby bunny in the weeds near the pond, and I brought him home. He had a bad cut on his leg, and Dad said it looked like he'd been attacked by a fox or a coyote. If that had been the case, it was amazing he'd escaped and was still alive. When I found him, his leg was all torn and bloody. I took him home, cleaned him up, and bandaged his leg. I kept him in a big box for a couple of months while he got better, and then I let him go in the woods. Or, I *tried* to, anyway. The problem was, by then he was too attached to me and wouldn't leave. I even tried taking him way back into the forest, but the next day he'd found his way back. I discovered him in our front yard, hopping around and chewing on grass.

So, he became my pet. I keep him in a big cage in our shed at night so he won't get eaten by predators. I let him out during the day, and he pretty much just hops around the yard. So, that's what I call him: Hops.

"Are there any fish in the pond?" Delaney asked, and she unbuckled her seat belt, slipped off the seat, and stood. She took off her helmet, spilling her long blonde hair over her shoulders. She was wearing a dark blue sweatshirt with a hoodie, as the October air was a little chilly . . . especially while riding in the off-road-vehicle. She placed her helmet on the seat and strode to the edge of the pond.

I, too, climbed out of the side-by-side. I unsnapped my helmet and took it off. My name—Jackson Porter—was stenciled in white paint above the brim of the helmet in large, cursive letters. Over the summer the paint had started to chip, and I planned to repaint it soon.

I carried my helmet under my arm as I walked to Delaney's side. "No fish in here," I said, motioning toward the pond with my hand. "Tons of frogs in the summer, though." I looked up at the gray sky, at the trees shuddering in the cool, fall breeze. It was autumn on Drummond Island, and many of the leaves had started to change color. Green leaves had given way to beautiful shades of yellow, copper, red, orange, and every hue in between. Many had already fallen from their branches, covering the ground like a carpet of colorful gemstones. The leaves that were still on the trees would soon turn brown and die, and be torn from the branches by fierce autumn storms.

"Lots of animal tracks here," Delaney said, squatting down on her haunches and pointing to the muddy ground near her feet. "Look at these."

I knelt down to see what she was looking at. There was a trail of very distinct tracks in the soft earth, creating perfect, tiny claw prints.

"Raccoon," I said, very matter-of-factly. Growing up on Drummond Island, I was very familiar with all of the various tracks left by the different animals.

"You can tell just by the tracks?" Delaney asked.

I nodded. "Every animal makes a different track, a different kind of print. See that over there?"

I pointed to yet another set of larger tracks only a few feet away, common tracks I instantly recognized. "That's a deer," I said. "This pond attracts all sorts of animals."

I stood and took a few steps to the left, following the deer tracks as they led to the edge of the pond. Then, they moved along the water's edge. I walked slowly, following them, every so often looking up to scan the bushes that crouched tightly around the pond. The tracks were so fresh that I thought the deer might still be around.

Delaney had moved in the opposite direction, walking the pond's edge. "Wow," she called out. "I wonder what made these tracks. They're huge. Are they from a bear?"

I turned and walked to her, stopping at her side.

I looked at the tracks in the soft earth.

I blinked and looked again.

I rubbed my eyes. Stared.

Delaney sensed my uneasiness. "What?" she asked. "What's wrong? Are they bear tracks?"

I ignored her. Not intentionally, of course, but I was too fascinated—too stunned—by what I was seeing to respond to her question.

These aren't bear tracks, I thought. My heart was racing as I inspected the tracks. *They must be wolf tracks.*

My heart hammered.

Wolf tracks?

Impossible. These tracks are bigger than my feet. Wolf tracks would be half this size. These tracks weren't made by a—

A tingle of horror slithered beneath my skin, wrapping around my muscles and flowing through my bloodstream. A terrifying, nightmarish vision came to mind.

No. No, it couldn't be. That's just a myth. A made up story.

Unless—

Just thinking the word in my mind sent a wave of horror streaking through my arteries, filling my heart with dread. My head pounded.

One word.

Just two syllables.

A two-syllable word made me dizzy with fear, icing my skin with terror-chill.

The word?

Dogman.

3

It had been some time since the creature had eaten, and he was hungry. He stood on all fours nestled in the pines near the pond. His body was relaxed but alert. Beneath his rough, wiry fur, tight muscles were unstrained but ready. Ready to spring, to run, to pursue.

Ready to hunt.

He sniffed the air with his sensitive nose. He was able to detect dozens of various scents, but nothing pleasing to his palate, nothing that would satisfy his hunger. He'd followed the scent of a deer to the pond, but the animal had been spooked and fled. A deer would have been tasty; a nice filling meal. But deer were fast, and required speed and effort to chase down. So—

He waited.

He listened.

Through the wind in the trees, another sound came. Although it was faint, it was unpleasant and irritating to the beast. It was a droning sound, steady, then rising in pitch, then falling.

And it was getting closer.

Still, he was patient, sniffing the air for any new smells.

Nothing.

Yet.

The sound drew nearer. Louder.

The creature bared his teeth, but uttered no sound. His muscles tightened, his eyes scanned the forest.

Still, the sound grew louder. The creature did not like the sound. It was noise, unwelcome and invasive. It made him angry. The noise was unnatural, mechanical, intrusive.

But the noise also meant—

Meat.

Food.

The beast turned, slinking along the side of the pond at an unrushed but steady gait.

And the noise drew nearer.

The creature, enormous in size even on all fours, slipped silently through the thick brush and crouched low. Peering through the branches, he caught a glimpse of movement. The sound of the machine ceased, only to be replaced by another sound.

Voices.

Humans.

Tucked in the shadows, hunkered to the ground, the beast watched.

And waited.

ABOUT THE AUTHOR

Johnathan Rand has authored more than 90 books since the year 2000, with well over 5 million copies in print. His series include the incredibly popular **AMERICAN CHILLERS, MICHIGAN CHILLERS, FREDDIE FERNORTNER, FEARLESS FIRST GRADER,** and **THE ADVENTURE CLUB.** He's also co-authored a novel for teens (with Christopher Knight) entitled PANDEMIA. When not traveling, Rand lives in northern Michigan with his wife and three dogs. He is also the only author in the world to have a store that sells only his works: CHILLERMANIA is located in Indian River, Michigan and is open year round. Johnathan Rand is not always at the store, but he has been known to drop by frequently. Find out more at:

www.americanchillers.com

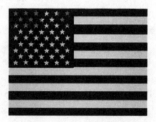

USA